SHADOWS
STILL
REMAIN

SHADOWS
STILL
REMAIN

a novel

PETER DE JONGE

HARPER

An Imprint of HarperCollins*Publishers*
www.harpercollins.com

SHADOWS STILL REMAIN. Copyright © 2009 by Peter de Jonge. All rights reserved. Printed in the United States of America. No part of this book may be used or reproduced in any manner whatsoever without written permission except in the case of brief quotations embodied in critical articles and reviews. For information, address HarperCollins Publishers, 10 East 53rd Street, New York, NY 10022.

HarperCollins books may be purchased for educational, business, or sales promotional use. For information, please write: Special Markets Department, HarperCollins Publishers, 10 East 53rd Street, New York, NY 10022.

FIRST EDITION

Designed by Eric Butler

All photographs by Daina Zivarts

Library of Congress Cataloging-in-Publication Data is available upon request.

ISBN: 978-0-06-137354-1

09 10 11 12 13   OV/RRD   10 9 8 7 6 5 4 3 2 1

For my father,
with affection and respect

. . . dusk do sprawl.

—JOHN BERRYMAN

SHADOWS
STILL
REMAIN

At 9:37 on Thanksgiving eve, nineteen-year-old Francesca Pena steps from the cramped vestibule of a crappy little apartment building in the East Fifties and hurries north. Model thin and shielded from the cold by only a vintage Adidas warm-up jacket, she leans into the icy wind that seems to hurl cars downtown and squints at the dreary commerce. This stretch of Second has never amounted to much. Tonight, with everyone on the way to families or bracing for their arrival, it's essentially shut down. The only exceptions are a candy store franchise that just changed hands and an Irish pub with an advertised happy hour that runs from ten in the morning to seven at night.

Pena turns west at Fifty-second and with long athletic strides traverses another cheerless block. She passes six-story walk-ups, a basement dry cleaner, another cheerless pub, and the headquarters for the Salvation Army. As always, she winces at the gap-toothed sign with its missing A's in S L V TION. An NYU sophomore on a track and cross-country scholarship, she has run through all kinds of neighborhoods, good and bad, but none as unsettling as this shabby bit of midtown fringe, where every endeavor feels dwarfed and mocked by the value of the real estate beneath it. As an antidote to the creepiness as much as the cold, Pena slips a chocolate malt ball into her mouth and picks up her already brisk pace. From Third on, the start of Midtown proper, there are no more random tenements or one-off businesses. There are only franchises and banks and office towers, and as Pena hurries through the emptied-out block, her bloodred jacket and short glistening black hair are the only colors. Thanks to the hotels, Lexington, at least, is well lit, and on the far corner is the glowing entrance to the IRT. When the signal turns, Pena bounds across the street and down the greasy steps, and after an expertly timed swipe of her Metro-card, pushes through the turnstile like a finish line. She barely has time to throw away her used-up card before a southbound 6 train fills the station, and when she climbs up onto Bleecker, she's so glad to be downtown, the air feels ten degrees warmer and for the first time in what seems like hours, she is aware of the night sky. Seeing that she has fifteen minutes to spare, she makes a quick detour to Tower Records, where she grabs the latest No Doubt CD for Moreal and the latest Britney for Consuela, and after enduring a withering eye roll from the pierced cashier, heads south again.

A topless Kate Moss, still freezing her tits off at thirty-one, presides over the intersection of Houston and Lafayette. Pena, very nearly as alluring, crosses under her, setting off flash-bulb smiles from the cabbies lined up at the BP station. Safely across, she turns east on Prince. She passes the side of a building plastered with posters for sports drinks, bands, and video games, then hugs the high brick wall that borders the cemetery from Mulberry to Mott.

Compared with midtown, Nolita is barely reduced by the holiday exodus. Cars and pedestrians snake through the clogged streets, smokers huddle outside the bars, and as always there's a crowd waiting to get into Café Habana. East of Elizabeth, however, the street goes black. On Bowery, the restaurant wholesalers are battened down as if for a storm. Cold, and anxious for her walk to be over, Pena turns east onto Rivington. Half a block later, at the end of a short tight alley, she spots her destination: the four-month-old restaurant/bar called Freemans.

2

Freemans, styled like a ramshackle hunting lodge, is packed to the fake rafters, but Pena's friends have staked out prime real estate at the corner of the bar. Like Pena, Uma Chestnut, Mehta Singh and Erin Case are NYU undergrads. Standing side by side, they are so photogenic and multihued that if you cropped out the three-thousand-dollar designer bags and serious jewelry, they could be showcasing their racial diversity for a college catalog. In a sense they are.

Pena's arrival sets off a high-pitched eruption of girly glee. When it subsides, Chestnut, who believes with some justification that she reigns over everything below Fourteenth Street, sets off a second by announcing "Cocktails!" Singh, who is taller, curvier and darker than Pena and possesses an equally electric smile, asks for a Sidecar, and the porcelain-skinned Case, whose pink cable-knit sweater is somewhat misleading, a Beefeater Martini—dirty. "Dirty indeed," says Chestnut, whisking an intentionally greasy bang off her forehead. "And how about you, Francesca?"

"A Malibu and Seven," says Pena. "You can take the girl out of the barrio, but you can't take the barrio out of the girl."

"Why would anyone want to," says Singh.

The girls present their fake IDs, and Chestnut places the orders, including her own signature Lower Manhattan. When all the cocktails have been mixed, signed for and delivered, Case carefully raises her tiny infinity pool of gin and vermouth. "To Thanksgiving," she says. "Everyone's favorite excuse for a five-day bender."

"And to all your relatives who got seasick on the *Mayflower*," adds Pena. This sets off enough laughter that cocktails have to be steadied before they can be sipped again.

Time flies. Particularly when you're young and beautiful and getting wasted. For four hours, the four pals don't stop cracking each other up, and while occasionally a brave boy dares to breach the perimeter, they mostly flirt with each other. And although Chestnut's father just had a retrospective at MOMA and Singh's is the largest commercial landlord in New Delhi and Case was raised like a hothouse flower in eighteen rooms on Park Avenue, it's Pena, the scholarship girl from western Massachusetts, who is the undisputed star of the group. It is her approval and messy snorts of laughter the others vie for.

Chestnut, Singh and Case have elaborate Thanksgiving dinners to wake up for the next morning. By 2:30 a.m., they're inclined to call it a night. But not the long-distance runner Pena, who by way of explanation nods discreetly toward an older guy at the end of the bar.

"Tell me you're joking," says Singh. "He looks like rough trade."

"Doesn't he, though?"

"You're coming with us if we have to drag you out," says Case.

But Pena crosses her arms and shakes her head like a stubborn toddler, and after a final flurry of hugs and kisses, Chestnut, Singh, and Case have no choice but to abandon her. As soon as they're out the door, Pena's posture stiffens. In the tiny bathroom near the kitchen, she splashes her face with cold water, and when she returns to the bar, so-called rough trade has strategically relocated to the neighboring stool.

"I've been watching you all night," he says. "Am I finally going to get a chance to talk to you?"

"Not tonight."

"Any reason?" asks the deflated suitor. But he does it so softly and with such diminished confidence that Pena, who had already turned to the bartender and ordered a Jack and Coke, pretends not to hear him as she takes the drink to a small table in the far corner. As the last customers trickle out, she sits with her back to the bar and nurses her drink for almost an hour. Finally, as a busboy gathers bottles and glasses from the empty tables, she pushes out of her seat and navigates the short alley to Rivington and the half block east to Chrystie.

At 3:30 a.m at the end of 2005, the corner of Rivington and Chrystie was still among the darkest and least trafficked on the Lower East Side. At 3:30 Thanksgiving morning, it might as well be the dark side of the moon. Pena knows there's no point even trying to hail a cab until she walks the two long

freezing blocks to Houston. After three queasy steps, she realizes she is about to pay the price for mixing all those ridiculous
cocktails, and crouches between two parked cars.

"You OK?" asks a voice behind her.

"Get the fuck out of here," she snarls, and retches some
more.

3

Detective Darlene O'Hara licks the cranberry sauce off her thumb and savors the penultimate bite of her homemade turkey sandwich. She is enjoying her modest feast in the empty second-floor detective room of Manhattan's Seventh Precinct, overlooking a windswept corridor of the Lower East Side where so much unsightly city infrastructure—including a highway, bridge ramps, dozens of housing projects and this squat brick station house—has been shoved against the East River. The Seven is the second-smallest precinct in the city, covering just over half a square mile, and the curiously exact address of the station is 19½ Pitt Street, but there's nothing half-assed about the institutional bleakness in which O'Hara has chosen to spend a solitary Thanksgiving.

O'Hara is thirty-four, with wavy red hair, raw, translucent Irish skin, that even in late November is sprinkled with freckles. She sits at a beige metal desk facing a wall of beige metal file cabinets. The light is fluorescent and the linoleum floor filthy, and behind her, facing a TV that gets three channels badly, is a lunch table littered with the Chinese food tins and pizza boxes that couldn't fit in the overflowing wastebasket.

The windows are filthy too, darkening an already grimy view of the Bernard Baruch projects across the street, but the layer of dirt doesn't keep out the cold.

O'Hara isn't the slightest bit put out by her surroundings or solitude. In fact, she welcomes the rare quiet. *It's like getting paid to think*, she thinks, and besides, she isn't altogether lacking in company. In the chair next to her, curled up in the deep indentation excavated by her partner's ample Armenian ass, is her fourteen-pound terrier mutt Bruno, his peaceful canine slumber punctuated by snorts and sighs and the occasional rogue fart.

In addition to the overtime, O'Hara is working the shift for the distraction. Two p.m. in New York makes it 11:00 a.m. on the West Coast. In a couple of hours, Axl, her eighteen-year-old son and University of Washington freshman, will be heading to the Seattle suburb of Bellevue for his first visit to his girlfriend's parents, and O'Hara pictures Axl, sprawled in his ratty chair in his ratty bathrobe, girding himself for five hours of hell (the father is a shrink, the mother a dermatologist) with black coffee and Metallica. As far as she can tell, a fondness for heavy metal is about the only attribute her son has acquired from her, not including of course his red hair and ridiculous name. In most significant ways, Axl takes after O'Hara's mother, Eileen. This is probably a good thing and, once you've done the math, not surprising, since his grandmother is the person who essentially raised him. You don't survive having a kid your junior year of high school without a great deal of help, and as O'Hara polishes off her sandwich she makes a point of silently expressing the thankfulness appropriate to both her circumstances and the holiday. Still, the thought of Axl spending Thanksgiving at a dining room table in a real house with a real family makes O'Hara feel like crap.

The first two-thirds of O'Hara's shift go as quietly as expected. She reads the *Post* and *News* and half the *Times*. At 3:15, she gets a call from Paul Morelli, the desk sergeant on duty. A rookie patrolman, named Chamberlain, just brought in a Marwan Overton, nineteen, on a sexual assault. Should he bring him upstairs?

"It's Thanksgiving, for Chrissakes," says O'Hara. "It's supposed to be a PG holiday—turkey, a bad football game, family."

"Well, who do you think filed the complaint?"

"Martha Stewart."

"Close," says Morelli. "Althea Overton, who in addition to being a junkie, prostitute and a thief, is also the suspect's mom."

"Well, OK then."

Minutes later, Chamberlain escorts the handcuffed Overton into the detective room. After O'Hara takes the suspect from him, Chamberlain lingers awkwardly by the door, like someone at the end of a date hoping to be invited in.

"I heard you actually volunteered to work the shift," he says. "I couldn't believe it."

Although O'Hara wears no makeup, rubber-soled shoes, and cuts her own hair, and obscures her generous curves under loose-fitting pantsuits and button-down shirts, she's not fooling anyone. Half the guys in the Seven have a crush on her, and the young ones like Chamberlain tend to get goofy and tongue-tied when they talk to her.

"Hopefully, you'll get out on time at least," says Chamberlain.

"Thanks," says O'Hara. "I'll take it from here."

O'Hara walks Overton to the far end of the room and puts him in the holding cell, where he slouches disinterestedly on the corner of the metal cot. Faithful to the fashion, everything Overton wears is three sizes too big, but in his case it only serves to exaggerate how small and slight he is. Overton, who could pass for fourteen, is barely taller than the five-foot-three O'Hara, and after looking at his tiny hands and sad hooded eyes, O'Hara guesses that along with everything else, Overton was a crack baby.

Not that any of this matters to Bruno. Since Overton was brought in, Bruno has practically been doing summersaults, and after Overton tells O'Hara that he's OK with dogs, Bruno races into his cell and greets him like his last pal on Earth, which, not to take anything from Marwan, is how Bruno greets everyone. Detectives look for the bad in people, the incriminating detail, the contradiction, the lie. Bruno is only interested in the sweetness and never fails to find it. Overton is so disarmed, you'd think letting Bruno into his cell was calculated, and probably it was, because twenty minutes later, when O'Hara brings him out of the cell, Overton waves away his right to an attorney without a second thought.

"So, Marwan," says O'Hara, "you going to tell me what happened?"

"I was having Thanksgiving at my grandmom's."

"You live with her?"

"In Jacob Riis House," he says, referring to the eighteen-building project where she and her partner, Serge Krekorian, get half their collars. "It was nice until my mom arrived and started begging for money."

"What happened then?"

"I knew she was just going to use, so I said no," says Overton, looking down at Bruno and scratching him behind the ear.

"OK?"

"She pulls me into my room and puts her hand inside my jeans, says she'll take care of me for ten dollars. I was feeling so sorry for myself, I let her. After, when I told her I wasn't going to give her any money and never wanted to see her again, she runs outside and calls for a cop."

Imagination-wise, thinks O'Hara, *the city never lets you down.* Practically every day, it comes up with another fresh, fucked-up twist. And although few of the surprises are happy, O'Hara is usually more fascinated than repelled, and almost always grateful for the front-row seat.

His Thanksgiving tale over, Marwan looks up from Bruno to O'Hara and offers a heartbreaking sliver of a smile. Everything about him looks too small and young, but his eyes are ancient.

4

The next evening O'Hara and Krekorian stand outside Samuel Gompers House, two blocks up Pitt Street from the station, just north of the ramp to the Williamsburg Bridge. In the sixties, when the neighborhood was undesirable enough for city officials to get away with it, they threw up eight thousand units of public housing between Pitt and the East River, and when they all go condo and their tenants get relocated like Indians to reservations, O'Hara and Krekorian will have to find somewhere else to make their overtime. In the meantime, they're paying a visit to apartment 21EEE, following up on a domestic abuse, the crime that keeps on giving. Since they'd prefer to arrive unannounced, they're freezing their asses off waiting for someone to step in or out through the locked door.

Shielding herself from the worst of the wind, O'Hara turns her back on the door and looks across Pitt Street. Facing the projects and their captive populace of thousands are a nasty little Chinese restaurant, a Western Union that cashes child-support payments and a liquor store named Liquor Store, with more bulletproof glass than the Popemobile.

"I haven't even told you about my latest Thanksgiving fiasco," says Krekorian, who is built like a fire hydrant, the swarthy skin on his face pulled tight across prominent cheekbones like a pit bull's. After four years as partners, O'Hara and Krekorian are deeply familiar with the toxic ruts of each other's dysfunctional lives. She knows that Krekorian only dates black women with two or three kids, and he knows that O'Hara hardly dates anyone, and the two indulge each other by acting as if their emotional cowardice is primarily due to the stress and fucked-up schedules of police work.

By now, O'Hara is well aware of how little regard Krekorian's family has for his unlucrative line of work. To her own family, O'Hara's becoming a cop and promptly earning her gold shield is viewed as a minor miracle, particularly after the untimely arrival of Axl. To Krekorian's parents, who squandered over one hundred thousand dollars to send him to Colgate, where he was the backup point guard on the basketball team for three years, it's a profound disappointment, bordering on disgrace. At family gatherings his younger brother, an investment banker, loves to underline this fact by talking ad nauseam about all the money he's raking in.

"What you say this time, K.?" asks O'Hara.

"Not a word, Dar."

"Wow. I think you had what Dr. Phil calls a moment of clarity."

"He went on and on about his bonus and stock options and being fully vested, and I just let him."

"Like water off a duck's back."

"Exactly. Not a peep. I just sat there with my mouth shut and waited until it was just me and him in the den."

"And then?"

"I hit him."

"Maybe I spoke too soon," says O'Hara, staring at her shoes, trying not to laugh.

"If he's going to make me feel bad, I'm going to make him feel bad."

"Exactly."

Finally, an elderly Gompers resident ventures forth into the great outdoors, and the two detectives slip in behind him. The elevator is open on the ground floor, and as the doors close in front of them, Krekorian flares his enormous nostrils to draw his partner's attention to the puddle of cat piss in the corner. O'Hara knocks on 21EEE and announces herself and Krekorian as police.

Dolores Kearns, who came to the precinct and filed a complaint on her boyfriend the day before, takes about a week to come to the door. Kearns wears nothing but a bathrobe, and her ample breasts spill out of it. "It took you ten minutes to put that outfit together?" asks O'Hara, but Kearns is no more put out by the arrival of NYPD than Chinese food.

"I was taking a nap," she says, music seeping out from behind her.

"With Al Green playing?"

"I haven't seen Artis since that one incident," she says.

"That one little incident," says O'Hara, "where he slapped you around and held a knife to your throat."

"Like I said, I haven't seen him."

"But if you do, you'd call us, right?"

"No question."

When their shift ends, Krekorian parks their black piece of crap Impala in front of the precinct house and heads to his own piece of crap Montero in the lot. O'Hara runs inside to use the bathroom before her forty-minute ride home. Slumped in one of the filthy plastic chairs just inside the door is a brown-haired white kid in a gray hooded sweatshirt about the same age and loose-limbed build as Axl, and when she gets back down the stairs she can't help looking at him again. Like Axl, he looks like the kind of shy kid who could sit there all night, before getting up and saying anything to the desk sergeant.

"How long you been here?" asks O'Hara.

"An hour. I need to report a missing person."

"Who?" says O'Hara.

"Francesca Pena. She's nineteen, a sophomore at NYU, five foot nine, short black hair, about one hundred eighteen pounds."

As O'Hara looks down at him in his chair, the kid takes out a well-thumbed snapshot of a very pretty teenage girl with long jet-black hair and bottomless brown eyes. "That's before she cut it," he says, touching the picture. "When she smiles, she's got a beautiful gap between her teeth."

"She your girlfriend?" asks O'Hara, looking wistfully over the kid's shoulder at the door.

"Not anymore. Just friends. That's why I wasn't that worried when she didn't come home Wednesday night. We're not a couple anymore. That's cool. But we had planned to spend Thanksgiving together and I knew she was looking forward to it. Now it's Friday, and she still doesn't answer her phone."

"You roommates?"

"No, I'm visiting. From Westfield, Mass. Francesca's from Westfield too."

A handsome kid, thinks O'Hara, *but with that fatal transparent sincerity that drives girls away in droves.* Wednesday night, Pena probably hooked up with someone sarcastic and cutting and didn't have the heart to tell him she was blowing him off for their Thanksgiving dinner. It's amazing how many girls disappear at the start of weekends and reappear Sunday night. But O'Hara brings him upstairs to the detective room anyway. Partly, it's because he's not Dolores Kearns, and she can't imagine him two days from now looking through her like a pane of glass. Mostly it's because she misses Axl.

Without taking off her coat, she sits him down by her desk, turns on her computer and takes down his information. Name: David McLain. Age: nineteen. Address: 85 Windsor Court, Westfield, Massachusetts. Since he arrived in the city, he's been staying with Pena at 78 Orchard Street, 5B. He gives her the numbers for his cell and Pena's.

"How long you been visiting?" asks O'Hara.

"Three weeks. I've been working as a barback a couple nights a week at a place on First and Fifth called Three of Cups."

"Don't you want to go to college yourself?" she asks, not sure why she's talking to the kid like a guidance counselor.

"Maybe. I had a pretty good chance for a soccer scholarship till I let my grades slip."

With his forlorn expression and downtrodden posture, McLain looks almost as pathetic as Axl after he got dumped by his first real girlfriend sophomore year. People outgrow each other. Sad as hell, but it happens, and for six months, Axl walked around just like this kid, with his head so far up his ass that eventually O'Hara had no choice but to stage an intervention. On a Friday afternoon, the last day before summer vacation, she picked him up at school and just started driving. Chugging Big Gulps and talking, they drove twenty-six hours before they stopped in their first motel. Five days later, they walked up to a guardrail and stared with their mouths hanging open at the Grand Canyon. Looking at McLain, she doesn't know whether to hug him or kick him in the ass.

"Is staying this long OK with Francesca? She didn't give you a deadline?"

"Not yet. I help out. I buy groceries. I clean up."

"Where'd you sleep?"

"On the floor in my sleeping bag."

He's as loyal as Bruno, thinks O'Hara. But who knows? Maybe he got kicked one too many times.

"When was the last time you saw Francesca?"

"About eight-thirty Wednesday night. She was meeting friends for dinner. Then they were going to have drinks at some new trendy place. Don't know which one."

"You know the names of her friends?"

"No. Never met them. I'm pretty sure she's ashamed of me. One is the daughter of a famous artist."

"So what did you do after she left?"

"Shopped for our dinner."

"Where'd you buy the stuff?"

"A twenty-four-hour supermarket on Avenue A around Fourth Street."

"What time you get there?"

"About one a.m., maybe a little later. I think I got the last turkey in NYC. Then I got up at seven the next morning and started cooking."

"Who taught you to cook, your mom?"

"You kidding me? My grandmother."

You walked right into that one, thinks O'Hara, and for a second feels as bad as she did about Axl's suburban Thanksgiving.

"Keep the receipt for the groceries?"

"Why would I do that?"

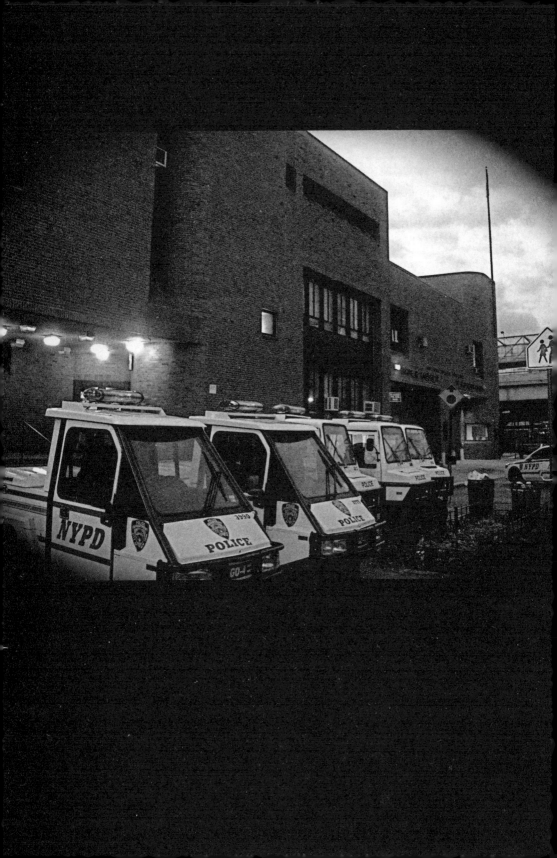

5

Saturday, O'Hara and Krekorian focus their crime-solving talents on a pocketbook, net contents seventeen dollars, snatched the night before at the Dunkin' Donuts on Delancey. When they get there, the manager has the whole caper cued up on video, and it plays like something out of *Oliver Twist*. The victim, African American, approximately thirty-five, sits at a table enjoying her coffee and the latest Patterson, when the five-foot, two-hundred-pound Astrid Canozares waddles through the door, a stroller in front and two hyperactive kids in tow. While the kids distract the mark, Canozares tosses the woman's pocketbook into the stroller, then mother, kids and infant, suddenly no longer hungry, exit the premises. O'Hara and Krekorian know the stroller is empty and the kids on loan because they've arrested Canozares three times in the last six months.

"The hardest-working obese kleptomaniac on the LES," says Krekorian.

"Hands down," says O'Hara.

Even though they know where Canozares lives, and the family that supplies the prop and extras, it takes all evening to track her down and another four hours to run her through the system. O'Hara and Krekorian share the collar, and because it's her turn, O'Hara gets the overtime, which is the only real point of the exercise, turning seventeen stolen dollars into an extra $176 on O'Hara's next pay stub. It's a long slow night, and O'Hara spends much of it thinking about David McLain and Francesca Pena, more worried about the lost boy than the missing girl.

Sunday, her shift starts at four, and in the dismal early dusk, the short thick precinct house, with its slits for windows, looks medieval. O'Hara tells herself she won't take the girl's disappearance seriously until the end of the day, but when she calls McLain and finds he still hasn't heard from Pena, she takes out her coffee-stained list of hospitals and ERs and starts making calls: Beth Israel and St. Vincent's in the Village, NYU, Cabrini and Lenox Hill, St. Luke's Roosevelt near Columbia, Mount Sinai in East Harlem and Columbia Presbyterian in Washington Heights. Pena hasn't turned up at any of them or in Hoboken or Jersey City, and near the end of their shift, she and Krekorian drive up to NYU to have a talk with Campus Security.

All O'Hara has to offer is that Pena spent the night with several classmates, one of whom may be the daughter of a famous artist, and Peter Coy, the new kid at Campus Security they got working the holiday weekend, can't do anything with that. O'Hara asks him to call Larry Elkin. Elkin is a former detective from the Seven, who retired from NYPD the day after he clocked his twenty years. A month later, he took a cushy security job at NYU. Now, still in his forties, Elkin collects one and a half salaries, and when he retires again, will do it on two pensions. If his kids are smart enough to get in, he might even get a break on tuition.

Elkin knows the friend, not Pena. "Uma Chestnut," he says when Coy hands her the phone. "Daughter of Seymour Chestnut. You may not give a rat's ass about contemporary sculpture, O'Hara, but NYU does, particularly when they go for fifteen mil a pop. First day of the semester, we get a list of every student whose parents' net worth is north of fifty million dollars. Someone says boo to Junior or Little Princess, we come running with our Tasers and mace. The amazing thing, Dar, is how fucking many of them there are, thirty, forty, in every class."

Elkin tells Coy where to find the contact numbers, and O'Hara leaves messages for Chestnut on answering machines at three addresses. While they wait for her to call back, she and Krekorian eat a couple slices in the front seat of the Impala and watch shaggy-haired college kids get dropped off by their parents after their first long weekend home.

"You look like them ten years ago, K.?"

"I don't know what I look like now."

"It's called denial."

What O'Hara looks for and can't find in the faces of the students is fear, not only the physical alertness that animates young faces in the projects but a fear of the future. These kids don't seem to have ever doubted that there's a spot waiting for them somewhere in the world. That alone makes them so different from herself at a similar age, she could be staring into a diorama at the Museum of Natural History.

When Chestnut calls back an hour and a half later, they're back at the precinct house, their shift nearly over. She tells O'Hara that she, Pena and two other students, Erin Case and Mehta Singh, spent Wednesday night at a place off Rivington called Freemans. The three friends left at about 2:30 a.m., but Francesca, who was interested in a guy, decided to stay. "Can you describe him?" asks O'Hara. "Not well—he was at the other end of the room and the place was packed—but I can tell you that none of us liked him. He was older, close to fifty, and looked a little rough around the edges. Mehta and Erin practically begged her to leave."

O'Hara and Krekorian drive to Rivington, double-park and walk down a short alley formed by the backs of several small tenements, and although the buildings themselves look real enough, the density of gritty urban signifiers (graffiti, fire escapes, etc.) is suspiciously high, and all are spotlighted. At the unmarked entrance, they push through a thick velvet curtain into a restaurant/bar art directed like the set of a nineteenth-century period play. Oil-stained mirrors, blurry battle scenes and portraits of soldiers, their gilded frames chipped and warped, hang from wainscoted walls. Displayed among them are the mounted heads of bucks and moose and a large white swan with collapsed wings that appears to have just been shot out of the sky. The place is too far from Washington Square to be an NYU hangout, and the crowd is older. Like a lot of the people roaming the Seven at night, they are enjoying that languorous ever-expanding limbo between college and employment. At midnight on Sunday, the place is packed. Krekorian clears a path to the bar and gets the attention of the ponytailed bartender. He only works weekends but retreats into the open kitchen and returns with a very nervous Hispanic busboy, who was on that night. Because O'Hara assumes the kid is working illegally, she doesn't ask his name, just shows him the freshman Facebook picture of Pena they got from Coy.

The busboy recognizes her immediately. He points at a table at the other end of the room. "She sat over there. It was late. I was already cleaning up."

"Was a guy with her?"

"No."

"You sure? We heard she hooked up."

"She sat alone for a long time. She was the last person to leave."

"Was she drunk?"

"I don't think so. She looked serious."

When O'Hara gets back to the car, she makes the two calls she has been dreading for different reasons all evening. The first is to Pena's parents in Westfield, Massachusetts. The second is to her useless sergeant, Mike Callahan.

6

Thumbing the photograph of Pena in her coat pocket, O'Hara follows Bruno's jaunty ass down the steep porch steps and doesn't correct him when he tugs hard to the right. For nearly five years, ending in her late twenties, O'Hara lived with a fireman in Long Beach in Nassau County, and even though he was kind of a mess and his lips spent more time attached to his bong than her, O'Hara adored him and counted herself happy. At least until the morning she got a call from his other girlfriend, also NYPD, who informed O'Hara that she was about to have his kid. A week later, determined to escape the incestuous grip of Long Beach, with its bars for firemen and bars for cops and bars for both, she rented the top floor of a white clapboard house on 252nd Street in Riverdale, just west of the Henry Hudson Parkway. On days off, she treats Bruno to a longer and more interesting walk, and when Bruno realizes it's one of his lucky days, the sawed-off mongrel pulls like a rottweiler, steam snorting from his nubby black nose.

Bruno drags his owner past a 1960s-era high-rise, then slows to investigate the rusty fence that surrounds some cracked tennis courts. High on the list of things that kill O'Hara about her dog is the power of his convictions. No matter how many times he's checked out a certain stump or tire or fence, he never phones it in. Every stop and sniff adds to his storehouse of canine knowledge. Every piss sends a message, and every time he scrambles out of the house and into the world it matters a lot, at least to Bruno.

The two skirt the neglected grounds of a once grand Tudor mansion, and rounding the corner, O'Hara catches her first glimpse of the Hudson. As always, she's delighted that's she's seeing it not from a public lookout on the Palisades Parkway but through a small break in the trees on a quiet street half a mile from her home. Still preoccupied by her cruelly inconclusive conversation with Pena's parents the night before—the father, who answered the phone, could barely get a word out, while the steelier mom clung blindly to what little hope remained—O'Hara follows her dog to the river. She lets Bruno root among the cold, damp weeds a hundred feet from the water before she pulls him out and turns him back toward home. As they climb the steep hill, the burn in her thighs reminds O'Hara she hasn't been to the gym in a week.

At home, O'Hara saws three slices off a stale baguette and puts on coffee and music. Ten minutes later, when she steps out of the shower, her hair is clean and all the pieces of modest domestic life are in order: coffee aroma wafts out from the kitchen, Bruno sleeps on his side in a circle of sun, and Heart's Ann Wilson sings "Crazy on You." When O'Hara moved in with the fireman, every bit of decor, not to mention his collection of piss-poor CDs, was all grandfathered in, and any input on her part was highly discouraged. That's why, despite the fact that she was almost thirty when she signed the lease, this is the first place that feels entirely her own. The purchase and placement of every stick of furniture, from the overstuffed whorehouse couch (a flea market on Columbus Avenue) to the small kitchen table (a Riverdale yard sale) to the brass floor lamps (IKEA in Elizabeth) represent an unfettered decision of one and give her inordinate pleasure. The same goes for the photographs, including the pictures in the small foyer of her parents and grandmother and Bruno. Her favorite, hanging just above the couch, is of her and Axl, in the midst of their epic road trip. It was taken at six in the morning in front of a motel in Fort Wayne, Indiana. Above them the sky is just lightening, and the fifteen-year-old Axl looks so beautiful and nakedly adolescent it almost feels wrong to look at him. As Axl and Pena and Pena's panicked parents clamor for different parts of her attention, Krekorian calls.

"Dar," he says. "You caught something big."

"Do I need to get tested?"

"Give me a call after you've seen the papers. I think we need to go in."

When O'Hara gets off the phone and fans her Monday papers out across the table, the same photo of Pena she has in her pocket stares back from all three. O'Hara is surprised the press jumped on the case so quickly. Being Puerto Rican and working-class is usually enough to keep anyone from getting much ink. But as O'Hara reads the stories, she realizes that Pena, with her wealthy friends and NYU scholarship, has the prospects of a well-off white or Asian kid. Plus, she's beautiful and light-skinned, and comes with an irresistible backstory.

The *Post* and *News* are interested in the potential tragedy as a cautionary tale. A teenage girl stays alone at a bar in the hope of getting laid. Therefore, she has to be punished. The *Times* concentrates on the poignancy of Pena's unlikely journey that began long before she got to NYU. Its story on the front page of the Metro section, above the fold, recounts how Pena grew up on public assistance in a notorious Chicago ghetto, lost her drug-addicted father to AIDS when she was eleven and got into enough trouble in her early teens to do two months in juvenile lockup. Desperate to escape the gravity of the inner city, mother and daughter rolled the dice and moved to New England. In Westfield, the mother was remarried, to a local carpenter and small-time contractor, Dominic Coppalano, and took his name, while Francesca kept the Pena of her late father. The terrified man on the phone last night was Pena's stepfather.

In the depressed former mill town of Westfield, Massachusetts, Pena rewrote her destiny, or at least tried to. She became a competitive runner and a motivated student, won a scholarship to a prep school and two years later a full ride at NYU. According to a quote from the assistant provost and director of admissions, Pena had made so much progress as a student-athlete, the school was planning to propose her as a candidate for a Rhodes scholarship.

O'Hara has read enough of these stories to know they're written to a curve. When catastrophe lurks, a pretty girl becomes a breathtaking beauty and a B student a future world leader. But it's the particulars of Pena's story that get O'Hara's attention. O'Hara also lost her father at eleven, and although getting pregnant didn't get her sent to juvenile detention, the special school for fuckups on East Tenth Street wasn't much better. And then there's the oddly parallel cross-country trips, Pena's mother grabbing her daughter and heading east, not long before O'Hara and Axl headed west. And weren't both mothers attempting about the same thing: to distract their impressionable kids with a change of scenery?

O'Hara should have known Callahan would call reporters, but it never occurred to her that they would bite so enthusiastically. Now that they've decided Pena can sell papers, it's become the kind of case that can launch a career. But not for long. If Pena's disappearance is upgraded to a homicide, she and Krekorian will only get to work it for seventy-two hours. Then it will be turned over to Homicide South, and for O'Hara and Krekorian, it's back to burglaries and domestic disputes, Astrid with her stroller and fake kids and Dolores in her bathrobe.

7

Krekorian lives twenty miles up the Palisades in the Rockland County town of New City, or as he likes to call it, Jew City. He picks up O'Hara on his way in, and they get to Freemans at 2:30 p.m., several hours before it's due to open. Although O'Hara finds the place a lot easier to take empty, the daylight isn't kind to the decor and reveals how little money was spent to achieve its faux-antique effects. The oil-stained mirrors and dusty paintings that at night suggested the lodgings and funky heirlooms of a hard-partying disinherited count look like sidewalk trash during the day, and the animal heads on the walls look like roadkill.

"Two things you can't avoid, Dar," says Krekorian, nodding at a glassy-eyed elk.

"Death and taxidermy."

"I guess someone forgot to tell Wesley Snipes."

They sit at the bar and sip their coffee, while in the open kitchen a line chef sautées onions and a busboy pulls oversized plates from a dishwasher. Over the next hour, the waitresses and other kitchen staff trickle in, the employees getting prettier and whiter the closer they get to the customers. The maître d' arrives, sporting a natty tweed blazer a couple of sizes too small, and soon after the weekday bartender, Billy Conway. "She was too pretty not to remember," says Conway, who actually looks like a bartender, with the thick shoulders and forearms of an ex-jock. "She and her friends had a couple spots at the bar. After they left, she moved to a table and stuck it out by herself to the bitter end."

"When was that?" asks O'Hara.

"About three-thirty. Because of Thanksgiving, we closed a little early."

"She leave alone?"

"Yeah."

"No one followed her out?"

"There was no one left to follow her. She was the last one here."

"She talk to anyone beside her friends?" asks Krekorian.

"Right after her friends left, a guy came over and tried to chat her up, but got cut off at the knees."

"You ever see him here before?"

"First time. About five feet ten, bad skin, long hair, at least fifty. One of those ugly Euro guys some girls can't get enough of."

"Little old for this place, isn't he?"

"Yeah, but we get a couple trawlers just like him every night. *Polanskis* we call them."

"Speaking of age," says O'Hara, "all four of those girls were under twenty-one."

"They had IDs; I looked at them myself."

"You should have looked harder. Polanski, how'd he take getting shot down?"

"Quite well. I don't think he was going to leave the country. Besides, she did it so fast, it was like laser surgery. If I wasn't right in front of them pulling a draft, I wouldn't have noticed. He finished his drink, put down a generous tip and left. Paid cash, or I'd look for the receipt. Then she took her Jack and Coke and sat down at that table."

"You remember every drink you pour four days later?" asks O'Hara.

"The reason I remember is because she and her friends had been ordering one labor intensive cocktail after another, stuff that's a pain in the ass to make. As soon as they left, she switched to something simple. I was relieved. The other reason I remember is because it confirmed something I already thought, which is that she didn't fit in with her friends. They seemed like brats. She didn't."

"Anything else stand out about the night?"

"How about a beautiful girl, the night before Thanksgiving, closing down a place alone. Isn't that weird enough? And it wasn't like she was drinking herself blotto. It was more like she had nowhere to go."

O'Hara takes Conway's cell number, and she and Krekorian walk back down the alley, where on second viewing even the graffiti looks bogus. Despite being filthy, the piece-of-crap Impala is a welcome sight, probably because it's the only place in the Seven where they feel entirely comfortable. Krekorian starts the car and cranks the heat, and they sit in silence, giving each other the space to think. A soft rain has begun to fall, and at 4:30 Rivington is already deep in shadows, the last bit of light falling out of the sky like a boxer taking a dive.

"Something's off," says Krekorian. "Pena tells her girl-friends she wants to stay and check out this hot prospect. Then, the minute he comes over, she shoots him down."

"I hate to be the one to break it to you, K., but a girl can change her mind at any time. Maybe Polanski looked even older up close. Maybe he had a creepy voice. Or worst of all, maybe he smelled bad."

"According to Conway, she didn't let him get three words out. At three a.m. people aren't that fussy."

"They are if they look like Pena."

"Then why didn't she leave? Why'd she stay and order another drink?"

Slushy rain slobbers all over the roof, and O'Hara tracks a fat brown droplet down the windshield. In front of them on the curb, a tall Nordic girl wearing a purple and white NYU windbreaker, maybe a member of Pena's track team, steps up to a light pole and tapes a picture of Pena over the sticker for a band called the Revolutionary Army of California. When the student moves on, Pena's brown eyes stare down at them from the pole. O'Hara thinks of that mangy elk head on the wall.

"I say we have another talk with your buddy McLain," says Krekorian.

8

They decide to leave the car where it's parked and walk to Pena's Orchard Street apartment, O'Hara glancing at her Casio so she can time the trip and see how long it might have taken McLain to get back and forth from Freemans. At 5:03, the sun's gone and few lights have been turned on to replace it, and when they reach Chrystie, the steel skeleton of a condo in progress called the Atelier looms behind them. To the east, all is black, as if the night had taken the old neighborhood by surprise.

They cross dark, skinny Rivington Park between a rubber-coated jungle gym and an overgrown garden, the damp air smelling of night and greasy egg rolls. Then two more dark blocks to Allen, past a Chinese nursing home and a boarded-up synagogue whose windows are shaped like the tablets Moses, the first cop, brought down from the mountain. The synagogue can't be more than a hundred years old, but here, where a century is as good as a millennium, it's an ancient ruin.

On Orchard, lights have been strung overhead to announce the start of the Christmas shopping season. As O'Hara and Krekorian take it south, the Indian owners in the doorways whisper "very good price" and draw their attention to the racks of seventy-nine-dollar leather coats lined up on the curb. Even ten years ago this neighborhood was filled with bargains, its small narrow stores so stuffed with inexpensive merchandise it poured out onto the streets. These two blocks of Orchard between Rivington and Delancey are all that's left, an anomaly in a neighborhood whose only purpose is to provide a backdrop of authenticity for fake dive bars, pricey restaurants and whitewashed boutiques.

Seventy-eight Orchard is halfway between Broome and Grand, on the east side of the block. Less then eight minutes after leaving their car, they step into a vestibule papered with Chinese menus and hike the old tiled staircase, the marble so worn it looks like soft dough.

The door to apartment 5B is unlocked and slightly ajar. When they knock and step inside, McLain looks up at them from a tiny couch. He has a paper cup in his hand, half a bottle of Jack between his hightops, and the room reeks of pot. The rich bouquet reminds O'Hara of the fireman, and although in weaker moments she still feels pangs for the treacherous stoner, she also misses the pot. For some unfair reason, the NYPD routinely tests for marijuana and the FDNY almost never does, so maybe she and the fireman were doomed from the beginning.

"Throwing yourself a party?" asks Krekorian.

"No," says McLain. "Just getting wasted."

"How long you been at it?"

"What day is it?"

"Monday, Chief."

"A while."

"Is there a bed in this place?"

"I'm sitting on it."

"Where do you sleep?"

"I don't."

"When you did?"

McLain nods at the purple sleeping bag on the floor.

"Your old girlfriend slept on the couch, and you slept beside her on the floor? That sounds like fun. And you did that for almost a month?"

"It's her place. She didn't have to let me stay at all."

"She ever bring home guys?"

"Twice."

"She make you watch?"

"She called from the street. I took a walk."

"An eight-hour walk?"

"Went down to Battery Park and watched the sun come up. I recommend it. It clears the head."

"Ever occur to you that your old girlfriend was trying to tell you something? Rub your nose in it so bad, you'd take the hint and leave on your own?"

"It's possible. But I don't think so. She was looking forward to spending Thanksgiving together as much as me."

"So that was the fantasy? You roast a nice turkey, and she realizes what a mistake she's been making."

"Basically."

On the way up the stairs, the two agreed that Krekorian would ask the questions and O'Hara would look around, but

McLain's responses are so guileless, Krekorian can't get any traction, and the place is so small and sparsely furnished, there's very little for O'Hara to look at. Against the wall behind McLain is a small table with two chairs, a dresser and a column of textbooks, but except for the iPod dock on the table and a small pile of wadded-up bills on the dresser, there's not a single personal effect. It looks like Pena moved in over the weekend, not four months ago. More troubling to O'Hara, however, is the fact that there's no trace of McLain's Thanksgiving feast.

"David," asks O'Hara, "you ate the turkey yourself?"

"Too depressing. I threw it out."

"How about the pots and pans?"

"I washed them."

"David, I need a list of everything you bought that night at the grocery store."

McLain slowly stands, toppling his bottle of Jack with his right sneaker, and at the same time that he reaches under the cushion of the couch and pulls out a scrunched-up menu like those all over the vestibule, he catches and rights the bottle with his left sneaker. This feat of stoned and drunken athleticism that impresses even Krekorian, a former hard-partying college point guard. The menu is from Empire Szechuan on Delancey, and running down the right side is McLain's twenty-one-item list in small precise green letters.

"Keep it," says McLain.

"You remember the total?"

"$119.57," says McLain, refilling his Dixie cup.

"Got a pretty good memory," says O'Hara.

McLain gives O'Hara permission to look into the barely filled closets and drawers, but they are no more revealing than the blank walls and furniture tops. The only thing of interest, at least to Krekorian, is a Nike sneaker box that Krekorian pulls out from under the couch. When he brings it to O'Hara in the bathroom, he dramatically opens the lid on two vibrators, a dildo and other novelty items.

"What's the big deal?" says O'Hara. "A girl's got to have her toys. If something were to happen to me, I'd appreciate it if you'd go to my place and throw out the box under my bed."

O'Hara has no idea why she said that. She doesn't have a dildo under her bed or anywhere else, but Krekorian's junior-high leering, just like the tone of some of the newspaper stories, ticks her off and provokes a knee-jerk protective response. Those stories seem particularly unfair now that it looks like the only reason Pena was stalling at the bar was that she didn't have the heart to face her puppy dog old boyfriend. Even after they leave McLain and hump down the stairs, O'Hara stays on Krekorian's case about it. "The way you showed me that box was classic. It's like you're fourteen."

"That's not fair, Dar. I was just surprised Nike made a butt plug is all. Who do you think they're going to get to endorse it?"

"Callahan," says O'Hara. "This is Sergeant Callahan from NYPD, and I'm here to tell you about a remarkable new product that changed my life."

Outside, the lights have come on and the slushy rain has turned to light snow, and in the soft light the profiles of the narrow streets, with their tenements and synagogues, can't look much different than they did a hundred years ago. A large pack of NYU students have walked down from the campus and poured into the neighborhood to pass out pictures of their missing classmate, and in their straightforward parkas and hiking boots, they resemble missionaries.

O'Hara and Krekorian walk back through Rivington Park. This time O'Hara notices the crude sculptures rearing up in the weeds like downtown scarecrows, and when they get back to the Impala, O'Hara sees that Freemans has spawned a retail outlet, located at the mouth of the alley, called Freemans Sporting Club. The window is dressed with the same kind of old-timey props as the bar, and in the corner a sign reads, TAILORED CLOTHING, BARBERSHOP AND SUTLERY.

What the fuck, thinks O'Hara. A condo called the *Atelier*. A store that sells *sutlery*. O'Hara has worked in the precinct for five years, but take away the projects on the perimeter and she could be in a foreign country.

9

Three hours later, just before midnight, O'Hara and Krekorian watch through the falling snow as hundreds of NYU students and faculty crowd under the redbrick overhang in front of Bobst Library. While more students stream in from all directions, those in front, closest to the glass doors, grab a lit candle off a long table and file into the southeast corner of Washington Square. The column moves silently past the leafless trees and white-limned statue of Garibaldi, and when a thousand candlelit faces surround the recessed circle at the center of the stone plaza, O'Hara and Krekorian leave their car to stand at the rear of the crowd.

Unlike the Lower East Side, Washington Square doesn't seem foreign to O'Hara at all. As high school freshmen, O'Hara and her best friend, Leslie Meehan, would often skip school and catch a train into big bad Manhattan. A sizable chunk of those happy truant days was idled away in this very park, drinking Bud out of paper bags and making out with older boys with sideburns and brave smiles. The first time she let a boy slip a hand between her legs was in the grass at the edge of the square, although when she thought back on it, it was probably she who took his hand and guided it there. Sex is the one realm in which she felt at ease from the very beginning, maybe because with your clothes off, differences in class and income and education seemed less important and the playing field almost level. O'Hara isn't so naive anymore. She realizes now that death is the only leveler, and although some of these kids will undoubtedly get laid post-vigil, it's the prospect of death, not sex, that's brought them into the park tonight.

At the center of the circle are five stone mounds often commandeered by tattooed jugglers, fire eaters and street comedians. When the crowd settles, some twenty students separate themselves from the pack, divide into groups of three and four, and climb onto the elevated platforms. Then a female student, small and blond, wearing a camel-hair coat, steps out from the crowd to face them. When she throws her arms into the air, twenty voices rise into the snow-filled night, and as O'Hara follows them upward, she looks north over the scaled-down Arc de Triomphe and elegant town houses just north of the park to the office towers of Midtown, where these same kids will soon be fighting hand to hand, cubicle to cubicle. In the middle of the dirge, which O'Hara is pretty sure is in Latin, her cell goes off.

"Darlene," says George Loomis, another detective in the Seven, "some skell in East River Park just stumbled on a body by the tennis courts. Me and Navarro are on our way over, but thought you'd want to know. The description sounds a lot like your girl."

10

Krekorian does a U-turn on LaGuardia, and with his siren pushing aside the sparse traffic, runs reds across town. Just short of the river, he takes the access road under the FDR Drive into the park and turns toward the pulsing lights in the shadow of the Williamsburg Bridge. East River Park is a narrow strip of public recreational space squeezed between the highway and the river that no one at tonight's vigil is likely to have set foot in, not because it's a wretched place, but because the highway cuts it off from the city. During the day, families from the projects take the walkways that cross over the highway into the park, but at night, it's a no-man's-land. If you're looking for a spot to dump a body, you could do a lot worse.

Krekorian drives south past the soccer fields and the baseball diamonds, and pulls in behind the squad car parked between the tennis courts and an overgrown bathroom. Whitewashed by a couple of inches of fresh snow, the park looks as good as it ever will, but the snow can't do much for the FDR over their shoulder or the black undercarriage of the bridge or the warehouses that form the Williamsburg skyline across the river. On the other side of the squad car, blocked in by a van from

Crime Scene, is a piece-of-crap Impala as filthy as theirs, and standing beside it are Steve Navarro, George Loomis and Russ Dineen.

Navarro and Loomis, who wear dark wool topcoats pulled off the same oversize discount rack, are fellow Seventh Precinct detectives who work the shift opposite O'Hara and Krekorian, and because this part of the park, the approximate latitude of Delancey Street, falls in the Seven, they got the call. The third, much smaller man, an unlit Camel bobbing precariously from the corner of his mouth, and wearing a leather jacket with a Grim Reaper patch sewn on the shoulder, is a medical legal inspector named Russ Dineen. Over the summer O'Hara and MLI Dineen worked on the suicide of a young female Indian intern. Before anyone bothered to pick up the phone, the body had been facedown in a tub for days, and thanks to Dineen, the straightforward but unforgettable phrase "Indian people soup" was added to O'Hara's lexicon.

Crime Scene has taped off a large rectangle around the bathroom, using the tennis court fence for one side. O'Hara wants nothing more than to duck under the yellow tape and see for herself if it's Pena, but etiquette requires that she first exchange pleasantries with the men who got here before her.

"Pretty horrendous," says Loomis, an even-keeled big guy not prone to exaggeration. "How long she been here, Russ?" asks O'Hara.

"It's been cold," says Dineen, and having squeezed whatever distraction he can from an unlit cigarette, finally cups his hands around it and fires it up. "Decomp is nothing like the summer, Dar. Based on color, smell, maggot activity and everything else, I'd say less than a week, but not much."

"That works," says Krekorian. "Pena hasn't been seen since early Thursday morning."

O'Hara takes out a copy of the picture on lampposts and doors all over the LES. "She look like this?"

"This girl doesn't look like anything, Dar," says Navarro.

"Whoever killed her had some fun first," says Dineen. "Rape probably. Torture definitely. She's carved up like a totem pole."

"Who found her?"

Navarro nods at the backseat of the squad car, where a man in rags is having a heated conversation with himself. "The plumbing in the bathroom hasn't worked for years, but sometimes the skels go in to get out of the weather."

"He goes by Pythagoras," says Loomis. "Last known address, the planet Nebulon. We'd talk to him but didn't want to interrupt."

"Fellas, I got to take a look," says O'Hara. "Me and K. been working this all day."

Whatever excitement O'Hara feels at the prospect of catching her first homicide turns into something stronger and murkier as she and Krekorian stoop under the yellow tape and inch into the bathroom. The body of a naked girl, encased in a pair of clear plastic shower curtains, lies on its side under the urinals. The two techs from Crime Scene, who stare at them unpleasantly from where they are stringing lights, wear masks, but the smell—equal parts excrement, decomposition and brand-new plastic—is not as foul as O'Hara had braced for. Much worse is the way the victim's final anguish is sealed and shrink-wrapped in bloodstained plastic. Her terribly constricted body is trapped exactly as the murderer left her, with her wrists bound behind her back and her legs bent slightly backward, tied at the ankles, her mouth sealed with tape, and her eyes wide open, as if still disbelieving what is being done to her. O'Hara feels as if she's watching the crime itself, not the result.

As O'Hara strains to take in the corpse in near darkness, the generator surges and the bathroom is flooded with light. Once her eyes adjust, she notices the missing tips from several toes chewed off by rats and at the other open end of the plastic tube, the missing tufts of short black hair. She now sees what Dineen meant by the totem pole. Livid circles cover the front of the victim's body from ankles to shoulder blades. Before the lights went on, O'Hara thought they were bruises, the product of a terrible beating. Now she sees that they are gouges, some an inch deep. And although, as Navarro said, the victim has been far too brutalized to resemble a snapshot taken in better times, and in the harsh light her skin is ghostly pale, the victim's height, weight, age and eye color all fit the description of the missing girl. O'Hara has no doubt she is looking at the body of Francesca Pena.

Technicians work the crime scene for hours, taking countless measurements and photographs. A team from Forensics dusts the bathroom door for prints, and an hour later a second team unscrews the door from its hinges and carts the whole thing away. O'Hara, Krekorian, Loomis and Navarro spend much of the night in the Real Time Crime Van. This recent addition to the NYPD motor pool is filled with hundreds of thousands of dollars of nearly useless customized electronics and computers, but at least the coffeemaker works. At 3:15 a.m. Navarro snorts derisively at the sight of a Jeep Wagoneer pulling up to the crime scene, and the four detectives try not to laugh as their sergeant, Mike Callahan, walks toward the van in cowboy boots and a brand-new leather bomber jacket.

"What are you two doing here?" he asks O'Hara and Krekorian, although the question would be better asked of him. "Busman's holiday?"

"O'Hara caught this as a missing person on Friday," says Krekorian defensively. "We've been working it as a potential homicide since Sunday."

"I guess you saw how the papers are running with it, so you know it's big."

Callahan, who made sergeant by scoring well on a test rather than distinguishing himself on the streets and augments his income by selling cop memorabilia out of his basement over the Internet, is the kind of house mouse no working detective has much use for, and O'Hara keeps her eyes moving in the hope it will make her disdain harder to read. She needn't have worried, because her sergeant's attention has already shifted to the black official-looking SUV that just drove up, and when Deputy Police Commissioner Mark Van de Meer steps out, the sergeant is gone without a word, ditching his detectives like four losers at a cocktail party.

"So long, Sarge," says Loomis under his breath. "It's been real."

Just before 4:00 a.m. TV vans from five networks pull up to the scene together. They've obviously received the same call from downtown, because five minutes later, the police commissioner arrives to do a thirty-second remote. O'Hara knows for certain the case is top priority when a third banged-up Impala arrives and Detective Patrick Lowry extricates himself from the passenger seat. Six foot five and nearly four hundred pounds, Lowry resides ambiguously in that gray area between fat and big, playing it either way as the situation dictates, and his eyesight has deteriorated so badly in the last ten years, he can't drive. And while both his epic size and his myopia have stoked the legend, as well as the fact that he was drafted out of Hofstra by the Philadelphia Eagles, there's no denying his résumé. Lowry made it to Homicide by twenty-eight and made grade at thirty, and every major homicide in Manhattan in the last twenty years has crossed his desk. Without saying a word to anyone, Lowry, with the help of his partner-chauffeur Frank Grimes, somehow gets himself under the yellow tape and disappears into the bathroom.

Across the river, a milky dawn puddles up over Brooklyn and Queens as Dineen and his ghouls load Pena into a van, and a grubby phalanx of Impalas follows it out of the park. Twenty minutes later, at the office of the medical examiner, O'Hara and Krekorian jockey for sight lines with Lowry and Grimes and two other homicide detectives. In front of them on a steel gurney, Pena, still bound and encased in plastic, lies on her side, exactly as she has since Thanksgiving morning. When O'Hara arrived, she saw for the first time that the back of the victim is also covered with gouges.

Conducting the survey of Pena's multiple wounds is a tall skinny thirty-two-year-old ME, Sam Lebowitz. As he circles the gurney, trailed by a forensic photographer, he jots notes on a long yellow pad, then reads them aloud to the detectives. "Lacerations and trauma on the back and top of the skull," he says, points at them with his pen, then backs up out of the photographer's viewfinder. "The skull does not appear to be fractured." Not to disturb a nearby colleague, who is performing an unattended autopsy of a middle-aged black man, Lebowitz makes his observations in a quiet conversational voice.

"There is extensive evidence of torture . . . The victim has been repeatedly and systematically gouged, cut and burned, front and back, from ankles to shoulders . . . blunt trauma around vagina, anus and inner thighs suggests rape . . . or multiple rapes."

After Pena has been examined and photographed on both sides in the condition in which she was found, Lebowitz, using long thin surgical scissors, cuts away the bloody shower curtains. When he peels the silver packing tape off her lips and removes the panties that had been stuffed into her mouth, O'Hara can see the gap between Pena's two front teeth that McLain couldn't stop himself from pointing out in his wallet snapshot that first night in the station house. Finally Lebowitz severs the plastic ties that bind Pena's wrists and ankles. *It's about time*, thinks O'Hara. But by now rigor mortis constricts her body instead, and untethering her limbs does nothing to release them.

"The shower curtains are an inexpensive common style and brand-new," says Lebowitz. "I'm not holding out much hope for them." He slips the four sections of shower curtain, along with the ties, tape and panties, into a large plastic evidence bag and returns to Pena for a second, less obstructed, tour.

"Closer examination of the head shows trauma was induced by a single blow from a small hard round object and confirms the lack of skull fracture. If the assailant intended to torture the victim, the limited damage of the blow may have been intentional . . . the body is covered front and back with approximately sixty gouges made with a crude serrated blade . . .

gouges range widely in size, shape and depth . . . body has also been repeatedly burned with a cigarette lighter and sliced with a second knife, although the number of slicing cuts and burns is significantly smaller than the gouges . . . the gouging alone would have taken several hours and caused considerable loss of blood, but not necessarily a fatal one, and although the victim has been subjected to overwhelming homicidal violence, there is no clear single cause of death . . . The lividity, or bruising, suggests the victim did not bleed to death . . . I think she was tortured until her heart stopped."

O'Hara likes the sound of the city in Lebowitz's shy voice and appreciates the way his mind and body work in sync— his cautious understated observations matched by the precise movements of his long fingers and hands. And unlike the ME at O'Hara's only other autopsy, it's not a performance. Lebowitz doesn't seem to be playing himself in an episode of *CSI*.

"There are abrasions and bruising to the victim's right wrist and abrasions to the fingertips and heel of the left hand. They could indicate the victim was dragged by her feet over pavement or other abrasive surface."

Having completed a second pass of the body, Lebowitz takes out a rape kit and does bucol swabs of Pena's vagina, anus and mouth, again noting the evidence of trauma to all three. He notices something caught in Pena's teeth and examines it with a magnifying glass. "Chocolate," he says, and scrapes it into another plastic envelope.

Lebowitz then takes a steel comb from the rape kit and runs it through Pena's pubic hair, which strikes O'Hara as longer and fuller than the current fashion. Lebowitz packs the comb in another plastic bag, then scrapes and cuts Pena's fingernails, hoping that like the pubic hair and packing tape, they may have snared some small part of her attacker. Having packed them away too, he points out the evidence of tearing in Pena's anus and vagina and the bruising in her throat.

To some degree, all this is preamble. The autopsy itself, which consists of the surgical removal and weighing of Pena's brain, heart, liver and other organs, is yet to begin. When Lebowitz makes a long incision just below the hairline on Pena's forehead and with a brisk tug peels back her scalp, all six detectives, from O'Hara to the most hardened homicide guys, have seen enough and head for the exit.

In the waiting area outside, a shattered couple occupy one corner. Although they are nothing like what she pictured, O'Hara knows they must be Pena's parents. Both are in their late thirties. The mother is tall and blond and looks eastern European, the stepfather compact and swarthy. His thick workingman's hands lie palm-up at his sides. Only O'Hara stops. She introduces herself as the detective who spoke to them on the phone a couple of nights before.

"I have a son about the same age," she says, "but I can't imagine what you're feeling. I promise you, we're going to find the person who did this."

Neither parent says a word.

12

From the ME's office, Lowry and Grimes proceed directly to the Seven, where Lowry commandeers the table in Callahan's office and calls in O'Hara and Krekorian.

"I hear you two have been on this for a couple days," he says. "What do you got for me?"

"I'll let O'Hara tell you," says Krekorian. "She caught it as a missing person Friday night."

"I don't give a fuck who caught it. I just need what you got. If anything."

Lovely to meet you too, thinks O'Hara as she flips open her notebook. O'Hara had been under the impression that for seventy-two hours the case belonged to her and Krekorian, but clearly that's not how it works when the media get this involved and a homicide gets jumped to the front of the line.

"The victim was last seen at three-thirty Thanksgiving morning," says O'Hara, reading from her notes, "walking alone out of a bar on Rivington between Bowery and Chrystie. A place called Freemans."

"They got bars on that godforsaken block now?" asks Lowry.

"Three," says O'Hara," unless they opened another this morning. Not to mention a store that sells something called 'sutlery.' "

"Military provisions," says Lowry. "Sutlery are military provisions. Who has her leaving that bar?"

"The bartender, Billy Conway," says O'Hara, pissed off at herself for bringing up sutlery and doubly pissed off that Lowry knew what it was. "Conway poured Pena and her girls trendy cocktails for four hours. At two-thirty, her friends pack it in, and Pena, who apparently was interested in a guy, stays. The hookup, as far as we know, doesn't happen, but she stays for another hour and essentially closes the place alone."

"So at three-thirty, our victim staggers alone onto the darkest block in lower Manhattan? Brilliant."

"Except for the staggering part. Conway says she wasn't visibly drunk."

"He would say that, wouldn't he?"

"So does a busboy we spoke to. Conway says that after her friends left, she switched from the fancy cocktails to a Jack and Coke and nursed it for an hour."

"Is that how you sober up, Red, with Jack and Coke?"

"I've done dumber things," says O'Hara, and feels a tap on her right foot from Krekorian, who is getting increasingly worried about the competitive edge to O'Hara's responses. The nudge takes O'Hara back six months to a night she and Krekorian spent at a beautiful old bar on East Eighteenth Street. The place is called Old Town, but because of the stained glass in the windows, the high ceilings and the cool wooden booths that feel like pews, they've renamed it the Church of the Holy Spirits. In the spring they often repaired there after night shifts, particularly lousy ones. On one of those nights, the foul residue from the shift led to round after round, and after three or four Jamesons too many, Krekorian directly violated their unwritten rule not to tell each other anything about themselves they didn't want to hear. "The problem with you, Dar," he said, "is you got a chip on your shoulder the size of an Armenian girl's ass." Krekorian wasn't telling her anything she didn't know. The attitude to which he referred had been there as long as her memory of herself, taking root when she was three or four at the latest, and had only gotten bigger over time. Nevertheless she was stunned, because to some degree everything else about her personality had been shaped in an effort to conceal it.

"Me too," says Lowry, "but I weigh three hundred and sixty, on a good day, and not even my mother thinks I'm cute."

That would explain it, thinks O'Hara, and Lowry flashes such a hard look, she wonders if she said it out loud.

"Anything else?" asks Lowry, still staring hard.

"After her friends leave, a guy or maybe *the guy* comes over and tries to chat her up, and according to Conway, she gently shoots him down. Again according to Conway, there's no drama, and the guy leaves an hour before she does, unfortunately after paying in cash."

"How about the ex-boyfriend who reported Pena missing?"

"David McLain," says O'Hara, "I don't think so."

"Oh really," says Lowry. O'Hara is not sure if she hears more sarcasm or condescension. Condescension, probably.

"Torturing someone for hours, then walking into the station and filing a report seems like a stretch for a nineteen-year-old slacker from Westfield, Mass., who'd been in the city three weeks. Me and Krekorian talked to him again last night before Pena was found. The kid's a mess, but he's not going anywhere. If he killed her, I don't think he'd stick around."

"That's all you got for me in two days?"

O'Hara makes a show of slowly thumbing through her notes one more time, and although they contain several more items worth mentioning, including Conway's observation about the unlikelihood of a beauty like Pena closing a bar alone, and K.'s related question about why she would stay even after blowing off the guy, O'Hara elects not to share them, telling herself a certified legend like Lowry would have picked up on such obvious irregularities himself.

"That's it," says O'Hara, closing her notebook.

"Then I need two things," says Lowry. "Her so-called friends in the precinct and the phone records for her last forty-eight hours."

An hour later, while O'Hara is still waiting on return calls from Chestnut and company, Krekorian brings over a printout from T-Mobile, and O'Hara can tell by the way he drops it on her desk, he thinks there's something in it.

"Between Wednesday night and yesterday afternoon, Pena got eleven calls—two from her mother, four from her father, and five from McLain."

"It's her stepfather," says O'Hara.

"Stepfather," says Krekorian, "whatever. The last incoming call she picked up was at eight-thirty p.m. Wednesday night from Chestnut," he says. "That checks with what you got from McLain about Pena meeting her friends at eight-thirty. In total, she got seven calls her last two days—two from McLain, two from Chestnut, one each from Case, Singh and her parents. Over the same period, there are five outgoing calls—one each to Chestnut, Singh, and Case and two to McLain."

"In other words," says O'Hara, "no calls to or from anyone we don't already know about."

"Yeah, but only making five calls in two days? For a nineteen-year-old girl? That's got to be a record."

"You read the stories, K. Practice, studying, volunteer work. Pena had a lot on her plate."

A little after four, Chestnut, Singh and Case arrive together, each chaperoned by a middle-aged male attorney. O'Hara clears the lunch table of debris, pulls up a couple extra chairs and is in the midst of thanking the debutantes for coming, when Lowry steps up to the table with his own chair and cuts her off.

"Was Pena having trouble with anyone?" he asks. "A student, a teacher?"

"No" says Chestnut, "everyone adored Francesca."

"Anyone in love with her, obsessed with her?"

"We all were a little," says Case.

As the girls respond to Lowry's question, O'Hara finds herself checking out the jewelry sparkling through their grief: the single-strand pearl choker above Case's cashmere sweater, the gold Cartier on Singh set off by her fresh burgundy mani-cure, and the gold chain around Chestnut's neck, which, like her ring, is so big it's probably meant to look fake. *If this is what these girls wear at nineteen, what the fuck do they step up to at thirty?*

"She dating anyone?"

"She was too busy," says Singh.

"So she just hooked up with strangers at bars?" says Lowry.

"What's that supposed to mean?" asks Chestnut.

"Well, that's why she stayed, isn't it? She often hook up with guys at bars?"

"This is bullshit," says Chestnut, looking at her attorney for support.

"No," says Lowry. "What's bullshit is your friends leaving you drunk and alone at a bar at two-thirty in the morning."

"None of us wanted to leave her there," says Case. "But we're her friends, not her parents. Besides, she wasn't drunk."

"How many drinks did you each have?"

"Four, five," says Singh. "But we were there for four hours. We met Francesca at ten-thirty and didn't leave till two-thirty."

"She say what she did before she met you?" asks O'Hara, earning a scowl from Lowry for interrupting.

"Trained on the track at Loeb gym," says Chestnut. "She ran fifty miles a week."

"What do you know about her old boyfriend?" asks Lowry.

"She never mentioned him," says Singh.

"David McLain, her old boyfriend from high school, had

been staying at her apartment for weeks. She never said a word about him?"

"No," says Chestnut, and looks across the table at her girl-friends.

"Maybe she was embarrassed about him," offers Case. "An old boyfriend from her old life. People are funny about stuff like that. I wish she had told us, though. It makes me feel terrible that she didn't think she could tell us."

"One last thing, ladies," says Lowry. "I need your fake IDs, all of them, right now, on the table."

When the meeting concludes, O'Hara and Krekorian walk the girls and their attorneys to the street, where three Lincoln Town cars are idling. After the limos pull away, they linger on the steps outside.

"McLain told you that Pena met her friends at eight-thirty, not ten-thirty," says Krekorian.

"I know."

"I think we got to tell Lowry."

"You think he's sharing ideas with us?"

"There's no *I* in *team*, Dar."

"Really? I never could spell for shit."

13

By the end of that night, Lowry has O'Hara and Krekorian out canvassing the block where Pena was last seen alive. Rivington, between Bowery and Chrystie, has a nightclub, a beer garden, an SRO turned discount hotel, two restaurant supply stores and eleven small tenements. Several have windows that look out directly onto the alley leading to Freemans, and all have either tenants, customers or employees who might have encountered Pena as she left the bar, or at least seen or heard something.

They start with the German joint, Loreley. At 10:30 the rough-hewn bar contains half a dozen men in multicolored football jerseys who sip from tall steins and watch a rebroadcast from the Bundesleague. It turns out that six of the nine employees who closed Loreley last Wednesday are working on this Tuesday night, and over the next two hours, the manager brings the bouncer, a waitress, a line chef and three busboys to his basement office, one at a time.

What time did they leave work? Which way did they turn when they stepped out the door? Did they notice a woman with short black hair coming out of that alley? Did they notice or hear anything unusual early that morning? A woman's cry? A scuffle? A car double-parked at the corner? Bouncers—steroid freaks and ex-cons, half of them working with phony IDs—are suspects by definition, but this one is a rabid soccer fan from Liverpool with a legitimate green card. When they run him through the new 9/11 computer at the precinct, he comes out clean, and like everyone they talk to that night, he has nothing to offer.

At 1:00 a.m., having gone without sleep for almost two days, they call it a night.

Six hours later, they're back on the same tight short block, knocking on apartment doors, Krekorian taking the buildings on the south side, O'Hara the north. It's tedious, unfocused gruntwork, like selling encyclopedias door to door or handing out leaflets for the Jehovah's Witnesses, and O'Hara is excruciatingly aware of her seventy-two precious hours of homicide time ticking away inside these poorly lit tenement hallways.

If the clock started running at seven yesterday morning when Pena's death was officially ruled a homicide, twenty-four hours are already gone, and it occurs to O'Hara more than once that Lowry is taking pleasure in the fact that she and K. are pissing away their time so far from the front lines. That's why she particularly appreciates the call she gets from Medical Examiner Sam Lebowitz later that night as she's descending a steep stairwell.

"I just spoke to Detective Lowry," says Lebowitz, "but I wanted to speak to you directly too. I'm sorry to say all the tests have come back negative. The only DNA we got belongs to the victim."

"You ever come across anything like that before?" asks O'Hara. "I mean after such a long messy attack?"

"More than you might think," says Lebowitz. "But it's always disappointing."

The tenements and the nightclub eat up all of Wednesday, which means that when they return yet again on Thursday morning, their homicide tour is down to its last twenty-four hours. They burn the first three of those talking to the employees of two restaurant supply stores and a fourth talking to the Indian manager of a small hotel, Off Soho Suites, whose tiny office still smells of breakfast curry. When they step outside, a tall man lumbers over in work boots. "I'm Charles Hall," he says, "project foreman for the Atelier across the street," and points at the building under construction O'Hara noticed several nights before. "There's something you need to see."

Struggling to keep pace with his long strides, they follow Hall to Chrystie, and then north under the scaffolding into the working entrance of the project. Just past the sentry box, Hall hands each of them a hardhat, grabs a flashlight and leads them through a maze of building supplies until they're standing in the southeast corner of the ground floor, facing the plywood sheets that separate the construction site from the sidewalk.

"Twenty minutes ago, a laborer came in here to get a ladder, and saw this spot here where the plywood had been pried apart by a claw hammer. His first thought was someone had broken in overnight or over the long weekend, maybe a junkie or some kids from the neighborhood. When I got here, I noticed these red spots on the floor and then this." Turning on his heels, Hall aims his flashlight at the cement floor, where a large broom appears to have been pulled through the dust. Stepping through open, wire-filled walls, they follow the trail as it weaves through stacks of steel vents and plastic tubing and large wire spools and ends at a stack of Sheetrock about two feet high. On the top sheet, the shape of a small person is outlined in dried blood.

14

O'Hara has Hall close down the job, then calls Jack Narin in Crime Scene.

"We got to tell Lowry about this," says Krekorian.

"No, we don't. It's our case for another seventeen hours and . . . twenty minutes. I want to let Narin take a look first. Maybe it turns out to be nothing."

"What are the odds of that?"

"How should I know? I'm not a statistician."

"Dar, you know that chip on your shoulder we talked about?"

"The one you compared to a prominent part of the female anatomy?"

"Well, guess what? It's even bigger than I thought. And it's about to fuck us both."

Narin and two assistants arrive in minutes, and starting at the same spot O'Hara and Krekorian did with Hall, they follow the track through the dust. Upon reaching the blood-stained drywall, Narin asks O'Hara where Pena was last seen alive, and when he learns that it was a bar around the corner, his assistants close the street between Freemans and the construction site. Lowry has other detectives out canvassing the blocks just east and west of them, and soon after the yellow tape goes up on Rivington and Chrystie, Grimes's Impala screeches to a stop in front of the Atelier. Lowry climbs out. "I just spoke to Jack Narin. He tells me you got a crime scene here. Pena's crime scene."

"It's possible. I didn't want to call you until I was sure."

"I assign you this block, and you roll your eyes like it's Siberia. It turns out, it's not a shit detail at all, and leads you directly to the goddamn crime scene. And you don't call me?"

"Like I said, I wanted to be sure we really had something first. I realize now it was a mistake."

"You're a strange bird, O'Hara," says Lowry, and if he didn't have far more pressing things on his mind he might speculate more energetically as to why this peon chick detective, who should be doing everything in her power to kiss his ass, is going out of her way to antagonize him. But seeing as he does, he turns his immense back and lumbers back to the car, which Grimes spins around so Lowry can address O'Hara one last time from the passenger seat.

"You want this crime scene so bad, O'Hara, it's all yours. Knock yourself out."

With Hall's help, Narin strings extra lights over the spot where the plywood was pried open and Pena dragged through, and works the crime scene backward toward Freemans. It's slow, tedious work, and when Narin can't tolerate any more of O'Hara's hovering, she retreats to what will soon be the Atelier's chandeliered marble lobby and huddles around a space heater with Hall and a still-annoyed Krekorian.

"Narin starts putting up yellow tape," says Krekorian, "and you don't think anyone's going to notice?"

"You're right," says O'Hara. "I owe you a drink . . . at least." To change the subject, she turns to Hall, who is slouching in a much too small plastic chair beside a laminated sign that lists the luxe features of the twenty-eight new units.

"Chuck, forgive my ignorance, but what the fuck's an *atelier*?"

"A studio or workshop used by an artist," he says. "It's a French word."

"OK," says O'Hara, pointing at the sign. "And what does that have to do with three-million-dollar apartments with Corinthian marble vanities and Sub-Zero refrigerators?"

"Fuckall."

In the midafternoon, Narin spots a tuft of black hair, the same length and color as Pena's, snagged on a nail in one of the scaffolding's two-by-fours, and an hour later, as the sun begins its precipitous descent, finds three drops of blood on the curb just north of the corner of Rivington and Chrystie. Based on the thickness of the drops and the tightness of the splatter, Narin speculates that Pena was crouching near the curb when she was struck, presumably from behind. Soon after, an assistant removes a nearby sewer grate and using a net at the end of a long telescoping pole, fishes an orange T-Mobile cell phone out of the muck along with an uneaten chocolate malt ball. As soon as they're found, hair, blood, phone and chocolate are driven uptown to the lab, and although the damage has already been done, O'Hara apprises Lowry in real time about each discovery.

When the sun drops completely, O'Hara notices the lights from the squad cars parked up and down Forysth on the far side of the park, and when she steps out of the construction site sees that cops are going door to door on Chrystie as well.

"They must be looking for security cameras," says Krekorian. "Trying to find a vehicle parked near here that night. Pena didn't get to East River Park by walking."

No wonder Lowry was so happy to turn the crime scene over to her and Krekorian, thinks O'Hara. Once the crime scene had been found, it instantly became old news, and he was on to the next step. An hour later, when Grimes chauffeurs Lowry back to the Atelier one more time and Lowry again extricates himself from the front seat, he's not pissed off. He's triumphant.

"Just to show there's no hard feelings," says Lowry. "I got something to share . . . At this point, Red, you're supposed to ask, 'What's that, Detective?'"

"What's that, Detective?"

"We just found video of a green piece-of-shit van double-parked twenty feet north of here on Chrystie from 5:20 to 6:05 a.m. Thanksgiving morning. At this point you're supposed to say, 'Congratulations, Detective.'"

"Congratulations," says O'Hara.

"Unfortunately, we only got the front of the van, and the camera angle is so fucked up, we can't read the plate."

"That's unfortunate," says O'Hara.

"Very good," says Lowry, "but the problem wasn't insurmountable, because we got just enough of a plate to see it was out of state. That makes me think of your pal David McLain, you know, the one you have such a good feeling about. So I run his name through the DMV in Westfield, Mass., and guess who's the proud owner of a green 1986 Ford Aerostar, if there's such a thing? That's right. We're heading over to pick him up now. Is there anything we need to know?"

"He's not armed, if that's what you mean. Can we follow you?"

"Why not? You can hear the little bastard confess."

15

The door to apartment 5B is still unlocked and partly open, and as far as O'Hara can tell, McLain hasn't moved in three days. He occupies the same spot on the couch in the same clothes, and based on the city of empties that has sprung up at his feet and the redolent cloud that hugs the ceiling, he hasn't given up Jack or reefer. When Lowry, beet red and sweating heavily from the five flights, approaches the couch, McLain tries to look around him to where O'Hara stands awkwardly in the doorway, but Lowry, who seems to fill the tiny room, moves to block his view. "Forget about her, David. Look at me. I'm Patrick Lowry, Homicide. You have to deal with me now. When did you get to New York, David?" McLain blinks at him through the smoke, and it's not clear to O'Hara that he understands the question. "When did you arrive in the city, David?"

"November fourth."

"How'd you get here?"

"Drove."

"What?"

"My van."

"What kind is it? What color? What year?"

"Aerostar, 1986. Doesn't really have a color. My guess is it used to be green. Why, you want to buy it?"

"Any reason you didn't mention the van to Detective O'Hara?"

"She didn't ask."

"Where is it now?"

"Tompkins Square. I scored a great space. I'm good till Tuesday."

"It's Thursday."

"Seriously?"

"We need you to show us where it's parked."

"I can tell you exactly where it is—Avenue B just above Ninth on the park side. The keys are on the table."

"No," says Lowry, lifting him off the couch by one arm. "You're coming."

Lowry stuffs him in the back of his car, and O'Hara and Krekorian follow them to Tompkins Square, where McLain walks Lowry to a sign reading NO PARKING TUESDAY AND FRIDAY, 9:30 A.M. TO 1:30 P.M.

"I parked it right next to this sign."

"Then where the fuck is it?"

"Someone stole it."

"No one steals a van worth forty-five dollars."

"Someone did."

Lowry shoves McLain back in his car, and O'Hara and Krekorian follow them to 19½ Pitt Street, where Lowry brings McLain up to the detective room and deposits him in the closet-sized box used for interrogations. To watch, O'Hara has to stand unpleasantly close to Grimes as they take turns staring through the portal-sized window in the door.

"We know you killed her, David," says Lowry.

"That's not true."

"You show up at her apartment, and three weeks later she's dead. You're the one who reports her missing, and best of all, we've got video of your van at six a.m. Thanksgiving morning, pulling away from the building in which she had just been tortured and killed. That's three too many coincidences."

"Why would I kill her? I loved her. She was my friend."

"But she didn't love you, David."

"That's probably true."

"Probably? We spoke to her friends. None of them had heard of you. You had been here three weeks, and they didn't know you exist. Francesca was embarrassed by you."

"Maybe a little."

"We know that she thought you were a loser. I bet she was afraid of you too. The last night of her life, she stayed at a bar on Rivington drinking alone till last call, anything not to go back to her apartment and you. When she left that night, she wanted you gone by the time she got back, didn't she? Is that why you killed her? Because she wanted you out of her life?"

Lowry is so tall and wide that most of the time, O'Hara can only hear McLain. Over the next three hours, he never asks for a lawyer or stops pleading his innocence. He doesn't even ask to be allowed to sleep. His only request is coffee.

At one point, however, he lifts himself a couple of inches in his chair and tries to look over Lowry's shoulder at the door. "I need to talk to O'Hara," he says, on the verge of tears.

"You can't," says Lowry. "And by the way, O'Hara thinks you're as guilty as I do. She has from the beginning. She's just been playing you."

"I need to talk to O'Hara," he repeats. On the far side of the door, Grimes stares disdainfully at O'Hara and puts two fingers together. "Your boyfriend's about this close to giving it up."

"Bullshit," says O'Hara.

"What was that?"

"Bullfuckingshit."

But when O'Hara peers back into the box and catches a glimpse of McLain's scared face, his features blur. For a second O'Hara isn't sure if she's looking at McLain or Axl.

16

At two in the morning, unable to watch any longer, O'Hara slips out of the precinct house and walks north up Pitt Street. She passes the shopping carts belonging to the skells who reside beneath the Williamsburg Bridge and Samuel Gompers House, the project that Dolores calls home, and doesn't stop until she reaches the corner of First Avenue and Fifth Street. That's the address McLain gave her for a bar he said he'd been working at called Three of Cups. Even though she's standing directly in front of it, it takes her a while to spot the steel stairs dipping beneath the curb to the basement.

Chris Rock used to do a bit about women needing only fifteen seconds to decide whether or not they want to fuck some guy. The first time O'Hara heard it, she laughed out loud because she knew he was right. O'Hara is the same way about bars and, to her surprise, hits it off with this one right away. She likes the purple felt cap, circa Sly and the Family Stone, 1974, jauntily perched on the head of the bartender, and she likes the band stickers plastered three deep on the ceiling, but mostly she likes what she hears: Aerosmith.

O'Hara grabs a stool at the bar and flags the barkeep, but

doesn't tell her she's a cop. "I'm trying to get in touch with a family friend. His name is David McLain. I was told he's been working here."

"David's a sweetheart. A couple nights a week he picks up empties and helps me out. Actually, I'm a little worried about him. He missed his last two nights, doesn't answer his phone. He didn't seem like the type to disappear without telling anyone."

"He isn't," says O'Hara, buttoning her coat to leave. "That's why I'm looking for him. I'm sure he feels bad about not calling."

"Can't I get you a drink?"

"Next time."

McLain told her the truth about where he worked. Hopefully, he told her the truth about his Thanksgiving shopping, too. Key Food, where McLain claims to have done it, is one block east and one block south, on Avenue A. When O'Hara enters the dated all-night supermarket, it's 2:50 a.m. Behind the Entenmann's rack is a ladder, leading to a tiny perch of an office where the manager works at a desk looking directly over the cash registers. The ceiling is so low, even the five-foot-three O'Hara can't stand straight. When the manager tells her he needs a couple of minutes, O'Hara sits on a milk crate and pulls out the menu from Empire Szechuan.

McLain's list runs in a thin green column down the right side. The first item is stuffing mix, and an arrow, shooting off it to the left, points to a sublist: chicken broth, mushrooms, celery, bread crumbs, pecans, eggs, sage.

For the past four hours, Lowry has been calling McLain a loser, and maybe, compared to a potential Rhodes scholar, he is. But how many nineteen-year-olds make their own stuffing?

After the detour for stuffing ingredients, the list continues: brussels sprouts, cauliflower, Yukon Gold potatoes, olive oil, chives, butter, cream, turkey (eight to twelve pounds), roasting pan.

The final item, added as if as an afterthought, is cranberry sauce, and, as with the stuffing, there's an arrow pointing to a sidebar: cranberries (one bag), apples (two), sugar, vinegar, ginger.

Ginger is the only item in the entire list that doesn't have a thin blue line running through it.

What the hell? thinks O'Hara. *The dude makes cranberry sauce from scratch too. Either he's perfect, or he's gay.* Her patience spent, O'Hara pulls out her shield and explains her need to verify a purchase made by a suspect early on the morning of November twenty-four.

The manager looks at O'Hara like she's nuts and he's busy. "How do you expect me to do that?"

"I got a list here of everything that was bought," says O'Hara, and holds up her Chinese menu.

"This is some kind of joke, right? Tell me, I'm being Punk'd."

O'Hara remembers that McLain also recalled the exact price of his purchases, and turning the menu over, finds it in her own handwriting beside the heading FRIED RICE: $119.57.

"How about if I told you the exact amount and approximate time?"

"That would help." Two minutes later, the manager points at the total on his screen: 119.57. Below it is every item on McLain's list that has a line running through it.

"What kind of supermarket," asks O'Hara, "doesn't sell ginger?"

17

When O'Hara returns to the Seven, the air in the room has gone flat and homicide detectives she's never seen before are sprawled at the desks normally used by Krekorian, Navarro, Loomis and herself. The homi guys look like salesmen stranded overnight in a small airport—Grimes's expression the sourest of all—and one look into the box at Lowry's massive sagging shoulders confirms that their prime suspect hasn't budged.

"Grimes," says O'Hara, turning away from the window and mimicking the way the detective held his fingers a millimeter apart. "McLain still this close to giving it up? Or were you bragging about your dick again?"

The homi guys, who don't seem particularly fond of Grimes either, find this highly amusing. Maybe Lowry hears one of them laugh, because seconds later, he storms out of the box. "O'Hara," he says, "where do you keep your civilian complaint forms?"

O'Hara points to the top of a filthy file cabinet. "Why?" Without responding, Lowry takes one and goes back inside, and from the small window, O'Hara watches Lowry slide the paper across the table toward McLain. "I'm tired of your cute bullshit," says Lowry. "Tell me what happened Wednesday night or fill out one of these."

"What is it?" asks McLain.

"It's a civilian complaint form. Here, you can use my pen."

Confused and scared, McLain looks at the form and then up at Lowry, who has taken his .45 from his holster and stepped to McLain's side of the steel table, where McLain's right wrist is handcuffed to one of the legs.

"What happened Wednesday night?" asks Lowry. "I don't know, "says McLain. "I've been trying to tell you th . . . ," the last part inaudible as Lowry pulls McLain's head back by his hair and shoves the gun barrel down his throat. "For the last time," says Lowry, "what happened?" McLain shakes his head and gags.

O'Hara waits for Lowry to put his gun away. Then she slaps the door and without waiting for a response, steps inside. "I need to show you something important," she tells Lowry, but doesn't let herself look at McLain. Furious, Lowry follows her out of the box into the short corridor, two mismatched bodies wedged into a space the approximate size of a phone booth, and stares incredulously as O'Hara hands him a printed receipt from Key Food.

"At one-thirty on the morning Pena was killed," says O'Hara, "McLain went to a grocery store on Avenue A and purchased twenty items for a Thanksgiving dinner for himself and Pena. At 1:55 a.m., when he walked out of Key Food, he was carrying $119 worth of groceries, including a ten-pound turkey, potatoes, mushrooms, pecans, cauliflower and brussels sprouts. There is no way on this Earth a guy buys brussels sprouts for someone at 1:55 in the morning, then tortures, rapes and kills that same person three hours later."

Lowry looks bad and smells a lot worse, four hundred pounds of fat-man body odor, spiked with rage. When he talks, O'Hara feels the heat of his foul breath on her skin. "O'Hara, I don't care if you're a vegan, an idiot or insane. You interrupt one of my interrogations again, I'll have your shield."

Lowry goes back inside and sits down across from McLain, and O'Hara returns to her post outside the door. But something in Lowry has dissipated, and just before six in the morning, he books McLain on a phony little marijuana charge and sends him to Rikers, figuring the place and its inmates can pick up where he's left off. O'Hara knows it's bullshit, but there's nothing she can do. She tries not to think about a soft teenage kid fending for himself in the city's biggest jail.

Nearly as hungry as she is exhausted, O'Hara drives to a diner on Second Avenue. From her crome-and-vinyl stook she watches the Hispanic cook calmly preside over five sputtering orders of eggs, one of which is her mushroom, pepper and onion omelet. The space behind the counter in which the cook has to maneuver is twenty-four inches wide and some fifteen feet long—*imagine a cop spending his twenty years walking a beat that size*—but O'Hara can tell he's happy in his work and gives his customers something more than just good food. She gratefully devours her perfect breakfast, then walks back to her car and sits in the sun behind the wheel. For the next forty minutes she slips in and out of sleep.

At some point during the night, O'Hara's seventy-two-hour tour with homicide came to an unmarked end. What she should do is go home to Bruno, drink a bottle of red and enjoy the most underrated perquisite of her sex, which is the ability to sleep uninterrupted for sixteen hours. Instead she drives west a couple of blocks and parks on Mercer just north of the Angelika Film Center.

When Pena left her apartment for the last time Wednesday night, she told McLain she was going to meet her friends for dinner. O'Hara already knows that's not true. The downtown debutantes didn't meet up with Pena until 10:30. Pena told her girlfriends that she had spent the previous couple of hours at the NYU gym, running laps on the rooftop track, and O'Hara can see a corner of the track from where she's parked.

O'Hara doesn't think that's likely either. If Pena was working out, she wouldn't have to lie about it to McLain, unless of course, being in her tiny apartment with her lovesick ex-boyfriend was driving Pena so crazy, she couldn't breathe. In that case, she might have said anything to get out, figuring she could decide what she was really going to do once she hit the street. O'Hara knows what that's like.

As O'Hara approaches the entrance, a student holds his ID up to a scanner and pushes through a turnstile, so it should be straightforward to determine whether or not Pena was at the gym. O'Hara shows her badge, and a guard walks her to a small office, where a student employee pulls a chair up to his desk. "People on the track team are here at all hours," he says. "What time do you want to check for?"

"About eight-forty-five p.m., last Wednesday," says O'Hara. "November twenty-third."

"Then I can tell you right now she wasn't here. That was the night before Thanksgiving. We closed the gym at five."

"Did Pena have an assigned locker?" asks O'Hara.

He glances at his screen. "One seventeen."

"Has anyone been here to look at it yet?"

"Not that I know."

The student pages a burly Polish custodian, who finds O'Hara a pair of rubber gloves and a plastic bag. Rather than going with her, which would require closing the girls' locker room, he gives O'Hara the master key. Number 117 is at the end of a row of full-size lockers allocated to varsity athletes. Several pairs of sneakers are piled at the bottom, and shorts, shirts, and running bras hang from the hooks. On an upper shelf beside some toiletries is a stack of expensive-looking envelopes, and when she pulls them down she sees that they've all been sent by one person. O'Hara carefully opens the top one. "I feel like I just got off a train at the wrong station and the joke's on me," she reads. "I think you made a hasty decision and you'll regret it, but right now all I want to do is fuck you, plain and simple."

The blunt, aching horniness of that last line takes O'Hara by surprise and reminds her that it's been too long since she's felt anything like it. Then she opens and reads the four remaining notes, which are just as direct and unrequited. All five are signed "Tommy."

O'Hara carefully slides them into the plastic bag and walks

out to her car. At this point, O'Hara is so exhausted she can barely see straight, yet one question bobs to the surface on its own. If Pena wasn't impressed by a guy who can make turkey stuffing and cranberry sauce from scratch, and wasn't stirred by expressions of honest heartfelt lust, what or who did she want?

18

Saturday morning, buoyed by a night and a half of dream-less sleep, O'Hara steers her Jetta onto the Henry Hudson Bridge and heads for lower Manhattan. With her homicide tour expired, it's back to the usual Seventh Precinct bullshit, but as O'Hara drives past the George Washington Bridge and the Seventy-ninth Street Boat Basin and the latest crap from Trump, she doesn't feel deflated. And when she exits at Twenty-fourth Street and flips open her cell and dials the number for the precinct, she understands why. She never in-tended to go back to work in the first place.

"I need a day off, Sarge," she tells Callahan. "I'm burnt to a crisp."

"Then take one, Darlene. You deserve it. More than de-serve it." If Callahan weren't such a useless prick, she might almost feel bad.

O'Hara continues east to First Avenue, her rattling Jetta showing its 97,000 miles, finds a space on Thirty-first Street and walks into the office of the medical examiner. Lebowitz's door is closed, and when she knocks, she hears a drawer slide shut before he tells her to come in.

"Working on your screenplay?" asks O'Hara.

"No screenplay," says Lebowitz as he opens his drawer and holds up the recondite medical journal he had been busted in the process of reading. If O'Hara is not mistaken, the thirty-two-year-old ME is blushing. "And I'm not consulting on *Law & Order* or *The Wire*. I'm the only one here who isn't."

"You don't like money?"

"Never had any, I wouldn't know. But I like my job as it is. I'm not trying to parlay it into something else. You here about Pena?"

"Yeah," says O'Hara. "I was hoping to take another look. I'm trying to make sense of all those wounds, the gouging in particular."

"It's an unusual way to torture someone," says Lebowitz. "And hard work."

As Lebowitz walks O'Hara down the hall, she gets her second surprise of the morning. Not only does Lebowitz blush and avoid eye contact, he moves well, like an athlete. In the morgue, he slides Pena's body out of her refrigerated locker onto a gurney and unzips the heavy plastic pouch. Seeing the ghostly Pena on her back, O'Hara is struck by the distinct halves of a long-distance runner, the torso spare and delicate, the thighs sturdy and powerful. "A pretty amazing body," says O'Hara.

"If you like skinny dead girls," says Lebowitz.

"The problem," continues Lebowitz, "is there are so many gouges, it's impossible to focus on any of them. Let's break her into quads and see if that helps." He pulls the top zipper down to the middle of Pena's neck and the bottom zipper up to her waist, so that only the area between her shoulders and hips is exposed. "This should make it less overwhelming."

On the front of Pena's torso, Lebowitz counts twelve gouges. "The wounds show almost no consistency," he says. "In length they range from six inches to an inch and three quarters; in depth, from over an inch to little more than a scrape."

Lebowitz then covers Pena's upper half and exposes her legs. This quadrant has fewer gouges (nine), and they're smaller and shallower. "The blade was getting duller," says Lebowitz, pointing at the rough edges. "The killer must have worked his way from the top down."

"And it looks like he was getting tired," says O'Hara. "The work is getting sloppier."

"Or maybe he's losing enthusiasm. By now the victim would probably have lost consciousness."

When Lebowitz rolls Pena over, they can see at a glance that the wounds on her back are larger and deeper than those on the other three quadrants, and the edges of the wounds are the cleanest, indicating that this is where the gouging began. "If someone was torturing someone," says Lebowitz, "you'd think they'd start on the front, where the victim would be able to see what was happening to her."

"Is there any way of determining which gouge was made first?" asks O'Hara.

"Not with certainty. But if I had to pick, it would be this one." Lebowitz points to a rectangular wound about the size of a credit card on the right side of Pena's lower back. "It's deep, and the edges look especially clean. The attacker clearly took his time with this one."

Lebowitz pulls latex gloves over his long fingers and with

a scalpel cuts a very thin slice from the center of the wound, places the cross section on a glass slide and walks it to a scuffed-up microscope on a nearby table. In high school, Lebowitz would have been the kind of nerd O'Hara would have shunned and, maybe even worse, given a hard time. But as he carefully takes off his wire-rimmed glasses, pushes back his dark unruly hair and bends over the eyepiece, O'Hara realizes she's become more open-minded. What she would like to do to Lebowitz now is stick her tongue in his ear.

"Sam?"

"What?"

"Thanks for calling me directly about the DNA and not just telling Lowry. I really appreciate that."

"I couldn't help myself," says Lebowitz. "I'm a Knicks fan. I root for the underdog."

"One other thing."

"What's that?"

"Before, when you said you didn't like dead skinny girls, were you just saying that? Or did you really mean it?"

"Every word of it," says Lebowitz, grinning but not turning from the eyepiece. "I'm a sucker for a pulse."

"One last thing, Sam?"

"What's that, Darlene?"

"You see anything in there?"

"Yeah."

"What?"

"Ink."

19

If you don't think women are suckers, check out the visitors waiting room at Rikers on a Saturday afternoon. The dingy space holds two hundred plastic chairs, and there's a dolled-up woman in every one. The only male visitors are babies and toddlers. These girls can barely keep their own head above water, and they've all spent way more money and energy than they can afford to put on a good show for some punk. Even their kids are decked out in miniature shearlings and Baby Gap.

In her standard-issue overcoat, slacks and sensible shoes, O'Hara is conspicuously underdressed, but most of the looks she gets are smiles, the girls assuming she's in the same leaky boat as them until a guard escorts her out of the room. "What about me?" shouts a girl who can't be more than nineteen. "I've been here two hours already. She ain't been here twenty minutes."

"She's a cop," explains someone smarter.

The guard leads O'Hara down a hallway smelling of watered-down cleanser and into a narrow room split in half by a Plexiglas wall. Inmates are on one side, their girls and babies on the other, and though the room is packed, it's remarkably quiet, everyone, even kids, doing their best to help their parents carve out a little privacy.

McLain's got a spot near the center of the room. When O'Hara sits opposite him, she sees the deep bruise above his right eye, the swollen lip and the cuts on the side of his head. The only good news is he's fighting back. The knuckles on both hands are swollen and raw.

"I hope you're holding your own," says O'Hara.

"Don't have much choice."

"Sorry about that," says O'Hara, "and sorry I couldn't do more at the precinct. But I got to ask you something—did Francesca have any tattoos?"

"Yeah."

"Where were they?"

"She only had one . . . on her lower back, off to the right. When she came home at the end of September, she had just gotten it."

"You know what it was?"

"All I remember is a big heart with an *S* inside, but I barely saw it. Francesca said it had to do with her father and didn't want to talk about it, which I thought was strange. I mean, don't get a tattoo if you don't want to draw attention to something. But with her father a junkie and dying of AIDS, that whole time in Chicago was pretty much off limits. So I let it go."

"Francesca ever mention a guy named Tommy?"

"Who's that?" asks McLain, struggling to keep the hurt from showing in his banged-up eyes and mouth.

"I don't know. I found a note in her locker."

When McLain shakes his head no, O'Hara takes a card out of her wallet and holds it to the glass. "I know the police got you a public defender, but here's one that actually doesn't suck. Her name is Jane Anne Murray. She's expecting to hear from you. But don't use my name on the phone. A detective will probably be listening to your calls."

20

New York Hardcore Tattoos and Piercing is bowling-lane tight and deep, and set up like an old barbershop. When O'Hara steps in at 9:00 p.m., prime time for a tattoo parlor, the only people in the mirror-facing chairs are the three tattooed employees. At the front of the shop, O'Hara scans a shelf of hardcore magazines and CDs by bands called Turnpike Wrecks, Last Call Brawl and Heartfelt Discord. Then she thumbs through the stockpile of designs, set out row by row on large laminated sheets, attached to the wall by a hinge.

The top sheet reminds O'Hara of those first cave drawings. Every creature in the food chain rates a design, although in the tattoo version a disproportionate number are rendered with a stogie jutting from the corner of their mouth. Others celebrate places of origin (Ireland, Puerto Rico) or institutions (the U.S. Marine Corps, Mom), but mostly they name the wearer's poison, be it cheap liquor, hard drugs or bad girls. And bad girls are overrepresented. A saucy vixen wearing fishnets, horns and a long red tail winks over her shoulder from the center of a page and nearby an angelic-looking rival dangles the key to the lock between her legs. As O'Hara jumps from a page celebrating noir chicks to one lined with gun barrels pluming smoke and knives dripping blood, she realizes that what she's really looking at is police work, or at least the incendiary crap that gets the ball rolling rapidly in that direction.

The detail, wit and imagination of many of the designs make O'Hara smile, and one in particular makes her laugh out loud, because it reminds her of that loquacious little Irishman Russ Dineen. It's a tat of the Grim Reaper, and obviously this one works the projects, because he's packing a .45 along with his scythe. To Dineen, who regaled O'Hara with tales of corpses frozen in the act of hiding their faces, or fighting off phantom intruders, the Reaper is just one more municipal grunt riding elevators and knocking on doors, and as real as the Con Ed meter man.

Eventually, a tattoo artist named Vincent gets off his ass and approaches O'Hara from behind. "Whatever you pick, you can't go wrong," he says. "On redheads the colors explode."

"Not quite there yet," replies O'Hara. "but I'm tempted. No shit." Instead of a wrinkled photo of a rose or butterfly, she pulls out her shield and a picture of Pena. She explains the reason for her visit.

"The girl's name was Francesca Pena. She was murdered last week, and we're quite sure the person who killed her cut a small tattoo out of her lower back. She lived around the corner from here, so maybe she had it done here. It would have been just over two months ago. The end of September."

Vincent checks his records and comes back shaking his

head. "We only did eleven tats the whole month. Even if she used another name, a pretty girl like her, one of us would remember her."

O'Hara isn't surprised business is slow at Hardcore. On her way back from Rikers, she stopped at her place and printed out the names of thirty-seven tattoo parlors between Union Square and Canal Street, and can't believe there's enough empty epidermis left to go around. Fanning out from Pena's Orchard Street address, O'Hara spends the rest of the night working through her list. She goes from tiny setups in the back of smoke shops on St. Marks to high-tech operations as chilly and antiseptic as operating rooms, but most fall somewhere between an all-night Laundromat and a dive bar. O'Hara is making stops well past midnight, and around 2:30 a.m., when the Manhattan parlors stop answering their phones, she crosses from Chinatown into Brooklyn and heads for Williamsburg.

Bedford Avenue is teeming, but the windy blocks by the river are empty. On a desolate warehouse-filled stretch of Wythe, above a basement entrance, O'Hara spots the skull, glowing orange like a jack-o'-lantern, and dangling from a creaking chain. Above it, swinging in the wind, is the crude wood sign for Bad Idea Tattoos.

Inside, the cicada drone of a working needle fills the air, and an enormous man, whose bald beige head is as festooned as Melville's harpooner, Queequeg, bends like a vampire over the pale neck of a skinny rock boy. A girl, every exposed inch inked and/ or pierced, greets O'Hara at the counter. She is no more than seventeen, as elongated and lovely as a model, and O'Hara tries not to wince at how efficiently she has rendered herself unemployable at anything other than what she is doing now.

"Theo," calls the girl, and the room falls quiet, as the tattoo artist spins away from his client and rolls up to the counter in his wheelchair. For the twentieth time that night, O'Hara pulls out Pena's picture, and Theo reaches for it with the biggest hand she's ever seen.

"I thought she might be a fainter," says Theo. "It was her first one, and she wanted it just big enough to read. But I was wrong, and the tattoo was right. That little girl had a lot of heart, not to mention a world-class Puerto Rican behind."

Despite his barbaric visage, Theo runs a tight ship and keeps a copy of every piece of work on his laptop. A printer spits out a facsimile of what he etched on Pena's backside. As McLain recalled and Theo alluded, the overall design is heart shaped. But that's not an *S* at the center, it's a *$*, and it's surrounded by six letters. The design Theo hands her looks like this:

The little lines, like quotation marks, rippling out on each side of the dollar sign, make the heart look like it's pumping money instead of blood.

21

O'Hara stuffs the copy of Pena's tattoo into her coat and steps back into the cold. The river is so close she hears it lapping against the breakwater, and looking across it, can take in the whole east flank of Manhattan from East River Park, where Loomis and Navarro found Pena five days ago, to the Triboro. *How about that?* thinks O'Hara. *The Brooklyn girl, who didn't even know she was smart until after she got kicked out of high school, knows something Manhattan doesn't. It makes the city look different.*

O'Hara knows the paper in her pocket is significant. If the killer intentionally removed Pena's tattoo, then maybe all the other gouges and burns are a misdirect, an attempt to make a coldly calculated crime seem random and psychotic. That could explain the discrepancy between the apparent rage of the several-hour attack and the lack of any DNA evidence. With McLain in Rikers, Lowry has expanded his search for McLain's 1986 Aerostar, sending NYPD detectives to Westfield and the surrounding areas and coordinating efforts with police departments in Boston and Springfield and Hartford. He even sent cops to Farmington, Connecticut, where Pena went to prep school. Take away McLain, and all Lowry has got is an opportunistic predator, someone who stumbled on a drunk girl on a dark corner and saw his chance. But if removing the tattoo was so important to the killer, killer and victim must be linked in some way. They can't be strangers.

Too amped to think straight, O'Hara races back across the Williamsburg Bridge. Homicide South is housed in the Thirteenth on East Twenty-first Street between Second and Third, buried in the back of the third floor in a space even smaller and filthier than the detective room at the Seven. At three in the morning, Lowry is the only one there. He sits at his desk and watches porn on his laptop, and although he mutes the moaning for O'Hara's benefit, he doesn't lift his eyes from the screen.

"Girl on girl," he says, "my Achilles' heel." O'Hara takes the copy of the tattoo from her pocket and drops it next to Lowry's laptop. "What now, more receipts for brussels sprouts?"

O'Hara knows she should grab her scrap of paper and bolt, but is too excited by what she's just learned not to share it, particularly since it proves her right and Lowry wrong. Stammering in her rush to get it all out, she explains how Lebowitz found that the first and deepest of Pena's gouges was the one that removed a tattoo, and also explains that she just got a copy of the removed design from the Williamsburg tattoo parlor where Pena had the work done. As O'Hara describes what she thinks it means, Lowry turns his attention back to his laptop and smiles appreciatively at the action. He never looks at the piece of paper.

"O'Hara," he finally says. "Every girl in America has a

tramp stamp over the crack of her ass. Let me guess—you do too? And what about the rape? Or should I say rapes? Were they misdirects too? A piece of advice, Red, and it's on the house: don't quit your day job."

O'Hara grabs the printout off Lowry's desk and humps downtown at a pissed-off, block-a-minute pace. She has no idea of her destination until she finds herself clambering down the steel steps of Three of Cups. The place is packed but there's a single empty stool at the end of the bar, and O'Hara is just settling into her spot when the bartender hoists a rusty old cowbell over her head, rings it a couple of times and announces last call. It's the same bartender who was working the other night, and O'Hara wants to ask her if she's familiar with the oeuvre of a band called Last Call Brawl, but decides that ordering three Maker's Marks and backing them up with three shots of Jaeger is pushing her luck sufficiently.

"I said I'd buy you a drink," says the bartender with a smile. "Not six."

"Don't worry, I'm buying. And yes, they're all for me."

"Been a long day, hon?"

"Yeah."

If something sad and slow were coming out of the speakers, O'Hara might do something embarrassing, like cry. Thankfully and somewhat appropriately, it's Humble Pie front man Steve Marriott screaming "30 Days in the Hole" like sixty would be better. And when it's followed by Skynyrd and Zeppelin, O'Hara wonders where this place has been all her life. When it comes to drinking, and it usually does, O'Hara and

Krekorian give the Lower East Side and East Village a wide berth. In the case of the former, they're abiding by the graft-fighting rule that forbids cops to patronize establishments in their own precinct, but cops ignore the rule every night and it's been ten years since anyone gave a shit. The real reason is those hipster bars, with their iPod mope rock, make O'Hara feel old and fatally uncool.

But this place plays the shimmering metal of her all-too-brief adolescence, with no apologies for the fact that it once got played on a million car radios and in one-hundred-thou-sand-seat arenas. *Obscure* doesn't always mean good, and *main-stream* doesn't always mean bad. At least it didn't back then. And if Axl Rose, Steve Tyler and Robert Plant are barely three degrees from Spinal Tap, fuck 'em if they can't take a joke. If you ask O'Hara, ridiculous hormonal posturing is half of what's *good* about rock and roll.

The first Guns N' Roses single, "Welcome to the Jungle," comes on. O'Hara, halfway through her second Maker's Mark, is transported eighteen years to a Brooklyn basement where a defiant fifteen-year-old girl was getting naked with Jimmy Beldock, a beautiful, charismatically pockmarked fuckup with too much balls to do anything but front a band.

O'Hara was born in 1971. Eleven years later, her father, who drove a truck for Boar's Head, keeled over from a heart attack. The next four years, her mom moved her and her brother every year, not when the neighborhoods got worse, but when they got too good to afford. That's when O'Hara started acting out, and by the time she got to Beldock's basement, she was exhilaratingly out of control, a precocious red-haired teenager and would be groupie-ready to party with anyone having the slightest connection to a band.

O'Hara feels like she discovered sex and rock and roll on the same night. To her, sex isn't like rock and roll. It is rock and roll. It's why she got preggers listening to Zeppelin in Beldock's basement, and why, when nine months later, three months after Guns N' Roses' first record, *Appetite for Destruction*, hit the stores, she gave birth to a sixteen-inch, seven-pound red-haired boy, she saddled him forever with the name Axl Rose O'Hara. And, thank God, he doesn't hate her for it.

Axl's unheralded arrival—no one had a clue he was in transit until the school nurse made O'Hara pull up her hippy blouse eight days before she gave birth—got O'Hara kicked out of high school and sent to a special school for fuckups, where all she had to do to collect her GED was show up and not get into fights. It also forced to her to calm down and start pulling her weight. Her first job was at a midtown travel agency, and the first thing she learned when she got there was that she was exceptionally competent, something no one had bothered to tell her in high school. Two weeks after she started, her boss gave her a promotion, and she'd probably be running the place or one just like it if her uncle, a retired transit cop, hadn't talked her into taking the police exam.

As O'Hara rattles the ice in her last drink, she wonders if the last eighteen years of semi-respectability have been a smoke screen. Maybe that arrogant piece of shit Lowry is right, and fundamentally she's still the same fuckup and loser the world declared her at sixteen. Maybe her "appetite for destruction" was never sated, and all it took was a little push to veer off the tracks again.

On the other hand, maybe she's been playing it too close to the vest, and what her life really needs is another infusion of rock. At the far end of the bar next to the door is a poster-size blowup of that famous photo of a thirty-two-year-old Keith Richards wearing a T-shirt that reads, WHO THE FUCK IS MICK JAGGER? No disrespect to the Stones and Sir Mick, but O'Hara's got a question a bit closer to home. *Who the fuck is Darlene O'Hara?*

22

Breaking in a new box of Advil is rarely attempted under happy circumstances. With the kind of hangover O'Hara wakes up with late Sunday morning, it's a gruesome exercise. By the time O'Hara rips apart the box, pries off the cap, deflowers the aluminum foil and plucks out the last shred of cotton plug, she's grateful her service revolver is in the bedroom. "Still feel like crap, Sarge," she says into Callahan's voice mail after she's washed down a handful. "Must be the goddamned flu." The first part is certainly true, the second unlikely, and O'Hara hopes the gratuitously colorful *goddamned* doesn't give her away. She couldn't have just said "the flu." It had to be "the goddamned flu." Fortunately Callahan isn't much of a detective. That's why he's a sergeant.

Gelcaps and coffee clear out enough space in O'Hara's head for her to rough out a working plan. If the killer knew Pena well enough to be connected to her by a tattoo, finding him is just a matter of learning more about Pena. You can cut out a tattoo but not every trace of personal history. As long as O'Hara keeps slogging forward, she's going to stumble on him eventually. She clears her kitchen table and plows through six days of unread papers, clipping every story about the murder and jotting down the name of every person with something to say about it.

Two stories quote a Dr. Deirdre Tomlinson, NYU's assistant provost of admissions. O'Hara calls her office, expecting on a Sunday afternoon to get another machine, but is startled by a booming theatrical "Tomlinson here!" Although Tomlinson was about to head home, she agrees to wait for O'Hara in her office. Based on the dramatic phone presence, O'Hara pictured a matriarch of some heft and vintage, but the woman who leads O'Hara into the parlor floor of a redbrick townhouse on Washington Square North is rail-thin and in her late thirties, her long skinny legs emerging from a chic tweed skirt and disappearing into knee-high equestrian boots. The unkind descriptor that pops into O'Hara's mind is "Condi with a 'fro."

"Francesca's death is a tragedy for her family and a catastrophe for this university," says Tomlinson, directing O'Hara to the high-backed chair facing her desk. "It's also a great personal loss. If there's anything I, or the university, can . . . do."

Despite her relative youth, Tomlinson's office is enormous. It's adorned with a dazzling array of African-centric art, and when Tomlinson sees O'Hara's eyes roving from piece to piece, the former literature professor plays the patronizing docent. "That photograph of a beautiful Kenyan woman was taken twenty years ago by a wonderful photographer named Irving Penn, and the small figures on the shelf are Ethiopian and fashioned, believe it or not, from cow dung. The collage of course is a Romare Bearden, one of our great late artists. It belongs to the university, obviously, but I get to look at it every day."

Cow dung is about right, thinks O'Hara, and does her best to keep her eyes from rolling out of their sockets. "It sounds like you knew the victim quite well," she says.

"I recruited her to NYU. The dean at Miss Porter's alerted me to Francesca when she was only a junior, and I visited her there as well as at her home in Westfield."

"Do you spend that kind of time on all your applicants?"

"Hardly. But Francesca was an exceptional young woman, and NYU wasn't the only school to recognize that. We had to beat out Stanford and Duke and half the Ivies. The good half."

As Tomlinson talks about Pena's lost potential, O'Hara revisits the elegant black-and-white photographs, and the ebony sculptures made of cow shit, and it all comes together. At the elite forty-thousand-dollar-a-year colleges, a qualified minority like Pena is the prize at the bottom of the Cracker Jack box, the one they all fight and drool over, and at NYU, Tomlinson is the designated drooler. "I'm going to need her entire file," says O'Hara. "Everything you got, from application to transcripts."

"I'm afraid I can't give you those. It would directly violate our confidentiality agreements." For the first time since O'Hara arrived, Tomlinson smiles at her instead of down at her.

"This has to be a PR disaster for NYU," says O'Hara, taking her time and almost enjoying herself despite the throbbing in the back of her head. "One of your most promising students has just been murdered. Not only that, she was raped and horribly mutilated. Every parent who is thinking of sending their kid here must be getting seriously cold feet. I know I would if I was in their position. Well, how do you think those parents will feel when they learn that the school and its administration aren't cooperating fully with the investigation?"

"Detective," says Tomlinson, teeth bared in what might be mistaken for a smile. "Do you always have a problem with women of color?"

Some folks, thinks O'Hara, *don't waste any time pulling the race card. Particularly ones who refer to themselves as "women of color." Sounds like a bad soul band.*

That's not to say Tomlinson is entirely off base. You don't grow up like O'Hara, broke and Irish in Bay Ridge, without a little redneck in you, and probably more than a little. And it doesn't help that Tomlinson is taller, skinnier and better dressed, with a Harvard PhD on the wall, compared to her own dime-store GED. But does Tomlinson really think O'Hara is going to admit to it? And what would it mean anyway? O'Hara doesn't say a word, just smiles back, and five minutes later, when she leaves Tomlinson's office and heads across Washington Square, there are two large folders under her arm.

In the gray afternoon light, the park looks nothing like it did during the snowy vigil. Both the grounds and demographic seem far shabbier, and no one in sight has anything to do with the university. Rosy-cheeked college kids have been replaced by people with not nearly enough money and way too much time, and the matinee crowds that have gathered around the malodorous dog runs skew heavily toward the gimp and insane. Dodging small-time pot dealers and clipboard fanatics, O'Hara walks the east-west length of the square, picks up a venti at Starbucks and enters Elmer Bobst Library, the red-brick edifice on the southeast corner. With its fourteen-story atrium, the balconies have become the favorite jumping-off points for student suicides—two in the last fifteen months— and as O'Hara crosses the checkerboard marble floor said to hypnotize the susceptible, she notices the Plexiglas barricades the school has built on every floor to thwart them. After she identifies herself as a cop, a guard tells her about the reading rooms on even floors. She gets off at twelve and takes a seat at an empty mahogany table, carefully placing her coffee on the carpet beside her feet. Floor-to-ceiling windows face north over the park toward Midtown, and far below through the leafless branches she can see the grid of sidewalks where a homeless man is moving in tight manic circles, the twelve-story remove turning schizophrenia into modern dance. To her right is a shelf lined with parliamentary papers documenting the British slave trade from 1866 to 1877 and by the entrance a cast-iron bust honoring an old dead rich guy named Charles Winthrop, whose estate must have picked up the tab for the room. O'Hara's high school years were a waste of taxpayers' money, and since then she has spent more time in dive bars than libraries. That ratio, however, might be subject to change, because the tranquillity, quiet and good lighting are all deeply appealing, and not just because she's hungover. While her young, well-heeled neighbors text and IM each other, steal music off the Internet and check the value of their trust fund portfolios, O'Hara puts her phone on "silent," takes a long sip of coffee and cracks the first folder. Soon, she is the only person in the room who is learning something.

Pena's application lays out the essentials of a two-part life that are as starkly different as the upper and lower halves of her own body. Her first twelve years were spent in Chicago, the next six in a small New England town, and her essay explains how she got from one to the other. In blue script, raw and ill-formed for a high school senior, she recounts how her father, Edwin Pena, a longtime junkie, tested positive only after finally beating his heroin habit, and died three years later on a cloudless spring morning. And just as O'Hara spiraled out of control when her father died young, so did the twelve-year-old Pena. Six months later, she was sent to a boot camp for troubled teens. Every morning started with a two-mile run, and Pena discovered her gift for endurance. Pena's mother knew a woman, more acquaintance than friend, who had moved to Westfield, Massachusetts, and that fall, determined to escape the old neighborhood, mother and daughter abruptly pulled up stakes. The only link between Pena's two lives was her new sport. In her first three races at her new high school, Pena finished eleventh, fifth and third, and the self-confidence earned on the track spilled over to the classroom. Two years later, the barrio girl reinvented as a student-athlete won a scholarship to a tony prep school for girls called Miss Porter's. At the end of the essay, Pena describes how events in her life sparked an interest in early adolescence, particularly that small window of opportunity, when a still impressionable young person can go up as easily as down. O'Hara knows high school seniors will say or write anything if they think it will get them into college. They're worse than drunk guys trying to get laid, but apparently, Pena actually meant it. Although her grades weren't as high as O'Hara thought would have been necessary to be considered for a Rhodes scholarship—one A-minus, four Bs and even a C—six of the twelve courses she took or was taking at NYU were in the psych department. Attached to her transcript is a proposal for independent study, already approved, based on her volunteer work as a mentor to two at-risk Dominican sisters, thirteen and eleven, who, like her, are the daughters of a recovered junkie. Pena, it appears, was a girl on a mission, the rare student who arrives on campus knowing exactly what she intends to do, and then follows through. But O'Hara knows that things are rarely as clear as they seem to a headstrong teenager. Not everyone can be saved, or even wants to be. Missionaries find that out all the time, sometimes by getting killed.

As O'Hara weighs the significance, if any, of Pena's sharply focused application and transcripts, a particularly annoying hip-hop ring tone shatters the silence. After much too long, a male student at the table beside her casually flips opens his cell "What up, dawg?" he says. O'Hara, who to her own surprise is already feeling proprietary about the thought-conducive quiet in old Winthrop's room, leans forward in her chair and whispers, "No talking in the library." Unfortunately, O'Hara's respectful reminder is ignored. So is the second, and the third is blown off from behind with a dismissive wave.

O'Hara quietly gets out of her chair and walks over to the

next table, where the student, about the same age as Pena, is still on his phone, still barking at his dawg. When he bothers to look up from under his gray fedora, he is stunned to see that a beautiful red-haired woman has taken the seat across from him. O'Hara stares directly into his eyes and smiles. Then she opens her coat and beckons him to peek inside. Now he sees the gold detective shield clipped to her inside pocket, and perhaps just below it, the black rubber handle of the .45 sticking out from its leather holster. "No fucking talking in the library," she whispers again, although at this point it's no longer necessary, and nodding at the likeness of Winthrop by the door, returns to her table.

When O'Hara finally descends from the twelfth-floor reading room, the lights have come on in the park. Checking her cell, she sees that Tomlinson has left three increasingly urgent messages, and by the third seems almost as agitated as the outpatient still turning tight circles in the deepening dusk. In a moment of weakness, O'Hara walks back around the park and deposits the folders directly into Tomlinson's skinny arms, although the assistant provost would have been less relieved had she known about the stop at Kinko's along the way.

23

The portion of 106th Street between Broadway and Amsterdam is a block going two ways at once—Caribbean nannies rolling $1,200 strollers west toward the co-ops and teenage moms dragging toddlers east toward the projects. No big mystery how it's going to turn out. Soon the only dark babies in the neighborhood will be adopted ones from Haiti and Ethiopia, but for now the rents are still cheap enough for Big Sisters to afford a storefront. The sign on the door says it's open Sundays, but it's closed for the night when O'Hara rolls up, her karmic reward for stopping to photocopy all those files. Although Big Sisters is closed, there's enough light from the street to see that it's run on a shoestring. Inside there are just a couple of old desks, a bulletin board, some beat-up chairs. When a truck stops on the corner, its headlights briefly illuminate a card table covered with candles, cards and flowers and above it a blown-up picture of Pena with her two little sisters. All three wear nice going-out clothes and beaming smiles. It's the third picture O'Hara has seen of Pena, but the only one in which she looks happy. On her way back to Riverdale, O'Hara grabs a slice near Columbia. Then she collects Bruno for his evening walk. As she trails the happy beast down the sidewalk, she calls Krekorian and leaves a lengthy message, filling her partner in about her visit to Lebowitz, Bad Idea Tattoos and Tomlinson. It's eight o'clock by the time she makes it back up the stairs to her beloved whorehouse couch.

O'Hara likes to think of her couch as a raft on which, like Huck, she floats downriver through an evening, book and beverage in hand, lumpus furrus at her feet, and every item of potential necessity (remotes, cell, laptop) safely stowed within reach. Despite all the grief she gives Krekorian for being a college boy, O'Hara is usually working her way through three books at once, and spaced along the backrest, like baited fishing poles waiting to catch a bite, are *Mortal Causes*, a Scottish mystery, *Garbage Land: On the Secret Truth of Trash* and *102 Minutes*. Tonight she concentrates instead on her stack from Kinko's, and out of respect for the still-vivid memory of her hangover, sips water instead of something red or brown. When the phone rings, it's Nia Anderson, director of Big Sisters, returning the call O'Hara left on her machine. "Sorry I missed you," she says. "Everyone's so depressed, we closed at noon. Besides, we're all going to the memorial tomorrow."

"I saw the candles and the cards," says O'Hara, "and the big picture on the wall."

"That was taken last month from our night at Bowlerama. Her little sisters are Moreal and Consuela Entonces."

"Did Pena connect with the girls through Big Sisters?"

"That's right—through our mentoring program. Pena began spending time with Moreal and Consuela while they were still living with their foster parents, Donna and Albert Johnson, but we introduced her to over a dozen girls and families before we found the right fit. What makes all this so horrendous and demoralizing for Big Sisters is that until three days ago, this was our great success story. Francesca didn't just mentor the daughters, but she inspired their mother, Tida Entonces, a recovering heroin addict, to get clean and earn them back. That's something everyone else had just about given up, including Tida. Maybe Tida manages to stay clean and the girls will be able to remain on track, but right now it all feels terribly precarious and beyond sad."

Anderson's heartbroken voice shames O'Hara off her couch and back across Spuyten Duyvil into Washington Heights. Entonces and her daughters live at 251 Fort Washington Avenue and 170th Street, a dark, forbidding building between 170th and 171st, a block west of Broadway. The neighborhood tilted Dominican twenty years ago. For the fifty before that, it was as Jewish as the Lower East Side once was, filled with German refugees whose old men and women never entirely lost their accents or regained their footing but whose children and grandchildren more than made up for it. The Dominicans aren't doing badly either. In less than twenty years, they have the toughest gangs in the city and control the bulk of the drug trade.

Tida Entonces is a large woman in a housedress and slippers. She leads O'Hara down the dark hall of an ancient railroad flat, seats her at the Formica-topped table in a fluorescent-lit kitchen, and pours her a coffee. The ravages of a twenty-year heroin habit are plain to see, but so is the intelligence in her eyes, the pretty shape of her face, the flicker of sensuality at the corners of her mouth. That might be the one bonus of getting hooked early. If somehow you can get clean, there might still be a little time left on the other side, and when her daughters, Moreal and Consuela, slip in and out of the room in a sad, shy daze, O'Hara can see that the squandered beauty of the mother has already started to bloom in her girls. Anderson described a fragile family that was just getting their legs under them, and it's reflected in the condition of the apartment, which is desperately spotless. For Tida Entonces, good housekeeping is not optional. The system is slow to take children from their mother and slower to return them, but when they have been lost once, the benefit of the doubt is gone forever, and losing them a second time is excruciatingly easy. As long as Entonces is lucky enough to have her children, she will be subject to unannounced visits from Children's Services. One failed drug test or the slightest evidence of backsliding, and her kids will be gone forever.

Entonces looks up from her coffee and attempts a smile. "I'd say Francesca was like family, but that's being too nice to my family. They never lifted a finger for any of us, but a young woman I had known two weeks decided she was going to save me. Even then, it was hard. After a twenty-year habit, I had all these excuses lined up in my head like toy soldiers—about why my life was hopeless, and why it was OK to keep using. Suddenly, those excuses were gone."

"How much time did Francesca spend here?" asks O'Hara.

"One weeknight she helped the girls with their homework. Then, every other weekend, she'd take the girls to a movie or a museum. Once, as a special reward, she even invited the girls to sleep over, then took them out to breakfast in the Village Sunday morning. 'We didn't have breakfast, Mommy, we had *brunch*,' they said. Everything she did was about showing them that there's a bigger world out there."

"When was the last time she was here?"

"Homework night was usually Monday or Tuesday. Because of the holiday she hadn't come since the Saturday before Thanksgiving. That's when she took them to the Museum of Natural History. See that?" asks Tida, and points at a plastic model dinosaur on the kitchen counter. "Francesca bought that for them on their last trip." Beside the dinosaur is a small white bag you fill yourself with a little plastic shovel at candy shops, and O'Hara remembers the chocolate Lebowitz found in Pena's teeth. "How about the candy?" asks O'Hara.

"From Francesca too. She was always bringing little treats by the house and giving them out as rewards."

"How did your neighbors feel about what Francesca was doing for your family? Any jealousy?"

"Nothing I noticed," says Entonces.

"How about the young men in the neighborhood? Any of them seem particularly interested in this beautiful girl? Anyone ever ask her out?"

"She was way above their kind."

"Wouldn't keep them from asking. Some of them must have been interested."

"When she visited," says Entonces wearily, "Francesca was just another pretty Hispanic girl. Believe it or not, there are lots of girls in this building just as pretty or prettier. The way she dressed and acted, no one knew she went to a fancy college or was so successful in her life. It wasn't anything you could tell by looking." Entonces stares into her coffee as if searching for something.

"Maybe she taught you enough already," says O'Hara. "Maybe you had her long enough to make it on your own."

"Detective, I'm thirty-three years old. If I look a lot older, and I know I do, it's because I was a junkie for so many of them. My best friend died in my arms, and I've seen people get shot dead standing closer to me than you are right now. But I've never been this scared."

24

Practice is making O'Hara a better liar. At 6:05 a.m. Monday, when she calls in sick for a third day, she eliminates the folksy flourishes and gratuitous colloquialisms and presents the untruth as simply as a piece of sushi. Then she pulls on stockings, her best dress and heels, and drops Bruno and a stack of CDs on the front seat of the Jetta. Pena's memorial starts at eleven, and MapQuest estimates the 218-mile trip from Riverdale to Westfield, Massachusetts, at five hours and ten minutes. I-95 is empty and the sun barely up as she motors past the exposed backsides of Stamford, Norwalk and Westport. They make such good time, they stop at a McDonald's near New Haven. There they both enjoy a breakfast burger, and afterward, the sight of Bruno squatting and extruding on the manicured sod beside the microphone causes the driver of a dark green Tahoe to roll up his window in midorder and tear out of the lot in disgust. O'Hara's cell rings as she's cleaning it up.

"What's going on?" asks Krekorian.

"Same old shit," says O'Hara. "Me and Bruno are on our way to Westfield for Pena's memorial, and the beast just dropped a McTurd by the express lane."

"Thanks, Dar. I get it. And I got something for you. This morning, I decided to go back a couple months in Pena's phone records, see if anything pops out. The first week in October, about the time she got her tattoo, she received twenty-one calls from Deirdre Tomlinson, the assistant provost of admissions at NYU. Nine were from her office, the rest from Tomlinson's home or cell. All of them were three seconds or less, half were hang-ups.

"That's interesting. At her office yesterday, Tomlinson took an instant dislike to me."

"Oh yeah. Sure it wasn't the other way around?"

"No."

"One other thing."

"What's that, K.?"

"When you have the flu, it's very important to drink plenty of fluids."

Saint Benedict–Our Lady of Montserrat Parish is a crucifix-topped 1970s A-frame with the spiritual gravitas of an International House of Pancakes. O'Hara grabs one of the last seats toward the back and anxiously scans the packed house. She's worried that Homicide sent a team to scope the room for possible perps, or even worse, that Lowry himself made the trip. But the only cops O'Hara sees are the contingent of gray-haired brass sent by the commissioner to demonstrate NYPD's commitment and concern. They're strategically deployed in the fifth row—far enough upfront to be visible, close enough to an aisle for a quick exit—and to her relief, they don't include anyone who might recognize a lowly detective like herself. In the middle of the front row are Ingrid and Dominic Coppalano. The wife drapes one arm around her shorter, darker husband, and from their relative size and complexion, O'Hara speculates that Ingrid Coppalano is the type of woman who keeps marrying the same man. Five rows behind them, O'Hara spots Dr. Deirdre Tomlinson and at the end of the same row, a man she recognizes as the president of NYU. O'Hara had hoped to talk to someone from Pena's time in Chicago, but in the whole church there are only three or four Hispanic faces, and all of them appear to be students from the second, sunnier, half of Pena's life, part of the large, well-scrubbed group who arrived in buses provided by NYU and Miss Porter's. The priest didn't know Pena or her family well and has the rare grace not to fake it. It's not necessary. A simple recounting of Pena's short life is enough to fill the room with sobbing.

When the priest concludes his service, O'Hara lets the crowd clear, then makes her way toward Tomlinson, who is still crying in her seat. "This is more than I can handle, Detective," she says. Working a funeral is questionable form, but unlike her colleagues, already halfway through their first round at the nearest tavern, O'Hara came here to learn something, not pay phony respects and tie one on. "Dr. Tomlinson, since we've got a quiet moment, I need to ask you about something my partner just brought to my attention. Going back through Francesca's phone records, he found that one week in early October, you called her over twenty times."

"I may have called that many times," says Tomlinson. "but I never spoke to her once. And she never returned my calls."

"Why were you trying to reach her?"

"I had a terrible feeling she was in trouble. I should have told you when you came to my office. I'm sorry."

"What made you think something was wrong?"

"Francesca had changed. It wasn't anything specific, but I could see it. When someone like Francesca turns her life around, the temptation to lose focus is enormous. A huge goal has just been achieved. You're nineteen, on your own in a great city."

"What are you talking about? I read her transcripts. Some of her grades could have been better, but I didn't see any backsliding."

"Maybe it was all in my head," says Tomlinson, on the brink of losing it. "I hope to God it was. Because that's what I told myself when I stopped calling. Now, it's obvious I didn't do nearly enough. I shouldn't have called twenty times; I should have called a thousand. I should have gone to her apartment and knocked on her door. I should have made her an appointment at Student Counseling and seen that she kept it. But what did I do? Nothing."

Tomlinson is gesturing so erratically that O'Hara fears a scene and backs off. She leaves the chapel and takes the stairs to the basement, where a modest spread has been laid out, and a long line snakes along three walls of the room as people wait their turn to offer condolences to Pena's parents. As in the waiting room at the ME's office, the stepdad appears eviscerated by grief. As her husband teeters beside her, Ingrid Coppalano handles the required interactions with neighbors and

students, and only the efforts of an attentive relative keep
Dominic Coppalano on his feet. With the other cops gone,
O'Hara joins the line and reintroduces herself. "I'm Detective
Darlene O'Hara from the NYPD. We spoke on the phone and
met briefly at the medical examiner's office. You must have
been tremendously proud of your daughter."

"You saw the turnout," says Coppalano. "They came by the
busload."

"It was amazing." says O'Hara.

"And it's not just the number," says Coppalano fiercely. "It's
the quality."

"Is there anyone here from your time in Chicago?" asks
O'Hara.

"Just me. When Francesca and I left Chicago, we vowed to
never look back. Only forward. Detective, do you know that
my daughter didn't just get into NYU? She was also accepted
by Harvard and Yale."

"No, I didn't," says O'Hara. "That's very impressive."

She clasps Ingrid Coppalano's hand one last time and smiles
sadly at her husband, who doesn't seem to see her standing in
front of him, then joins the crowd filing from the church. The
southern New England afternoon has turned bitterly cold, and
an icy wind blows through O'Hara's thin dress coat as she hurries toward her car and leashes Bruno for his walk. On the
far side of the street, across from the entrance to the parking
lot, a gaunt figure in an awful plaid suit stares forlornly at the
church. Only when Bruno tugs inquisitively in his direction
does O'Hara recognize David McLain.

25

"David," asks O'Hara, "why are you paying your respects from across the street?"

"Because I wasn't welcome inside."

"Francesca's family, they think you were involved in her death?"

"It's got nothing to do with that," says McLain, a beat-up ten-speed lying at his feet. "Her mom disapproved of me from the beginning. I can't really blame her. Francesca was going someplace. She didn't need someone like me. Thanks anyway for the lawyer. She got me released yesterday morning. I hitch-hiked here last night."

McLain says he's heading back to the city, and O'Hara offers him a ride. First, he has to stop at home, and when his bike won't fit in the trunk, O'Hara and Bruno trail behind him in the Jetta as McLain, doing nearly thirty with his hands in his pockets and tie flying back over his shoulder, leads them through a modest but tidy suburban neighborhood. In the middle of a curve, McLain casually pulls one hand from his pocket and points to a white mailbox with COPPALANO painted across it. Behind it is a small ranch house, a pickup in the driveway. After McLain crests a hill and crosses Main Street, the houses and yards get shabbier. He leads them past a rundown garden apartment complex and a boarded-up grammar school, then, pedaling furiously, turns off the road into a trailer park, where he drops his bike in the dirt and runs into a double-wide on green cinder blocks. O'Hara looks at the trailer and junk-strewn yard, puts it together with Ingrid Coppalano's bizarre comments about her murdered daughter's college acceptances, and isn't surprised McLain wasn't welcome at the memorial. Three minutes later, still in his pathetic suit, McLain steps out of the trailer toting a Hefty bag of clothes. Behind him, a woman waves from the doorway. "Shouldn't I say hi to your mom?" asks O'Hara. "Please, let's just go," says McLain. "She's half in the bag already."

On the highway, O'Hara asks McLain what he knows about Francesca's life in Chicago. "Next to nothing," says McLain. "She never talked about it, and I got the feeling the whole subject was off limits." The sun drops quickly, and except for the occasional snore from McLain and sigh from Bruno, the car falls silent. McLain is all arms and legs, and seeing him folded into the front seat makes O'Hara think of Axl and their great road trip of 2003. The week is so precious to O'Hara because it's the only example of bona fide parenting she's got to hold up and hang on to. As she ferries her sleeping passengers toward the city, she thinks about Tomlinson's hysterical premonitions and Ingrid and Francesca's shotgun exit from Chicago. She wonders if there was something about mother and daughter's old life that couldn't be outrun.

It's not quite seven when O'Hara pulls to a stop in front of a fire hydrant on Fifty-first and Ninth across from the building where a friend of McLain's has offered his couch. McLain groggily thanks her for the ride and grabs his clothes. O'Hara, exhausted and hungry, scans the block for a cheap restaurant. There's a falafel joint on the corner, Chinese two doors down, and as she reaches into the backseat for her coat, McLain steps back out of the apartment building. When he runs across the street and walks briskly down the avenue, O'Hara drops her police placard on the dash and follows him on foot. McLain weaves through the thickening crowds of the theater district, but thanks to his ridiculous suit, O'Hara has little trouble keeping him in sight. At Fiftieth and Eighth Avenue, she follows him down into the subway and onto a packed 1 train; four stops later, she follows him off at Twenty-third Street, where McLain turns west and picks up the pace. His long, loose strides eat up the wide crosstown blocks, and O'Hara curses her wobbly heels. By Tenth, she's a block behind, and when she reaches the isolated garages and storage spaces just short of Eleventh, McLain has vanished.

Across Eleventh Avenue, a soccer game is in progress on the well-lit Astroturf soccer field, and beyond that across the West Side Highway is Chelsea Piers. McLain might have headed for either, and as O'Hara weighs which is more likely, the side door of the strip club across the street crashes open, and McLain, propelled by an enormous tuxedoed bouncer, flies through it. McLain's momentum sends him staggering backward into a small vacant lot, where he trips and falls into an oil-filled puddle. O'Hara fears that McLain will not have the good sense to keep his mouth shut, and she's right. He springs to his feet and points at his soiled pants and torn jacket as if he bought them that morning at Bergdorf's, and whatever he shouts is all the excuse the bouncer needs to charge back through the door like an enraged bull. Instinctively, O'Hara pulls her gun and her badge, but as she steps into the street, she is cut off by a van pulling out of the garage behind her. By the time it clears, the bouncer is practically on top of McLain. O'Hara can do nothing but watch as McLain twists, tilts and kicks the bouncer in the face. The impact is so solid, it echoes off the walls, and the well-dressed behemoth stops in his tracks and topples over like a black refrigerator. Laid out on his back, he offers no resistance as McLain reaches into his shiny jacket and empties his wallet, and although it's not the response to a violent mugging taught at the academy, O'Hara returns her gun to its holster and smiles.

Money talks. Bullshit walks. Suddenly flush, McLain straightens his tie and hails a cab, and O'Hara, her blistered feet in agony, gratefully does the same. McLain's cab exits the West Side Highway at Fourteenth, and O'Hara, staying a couple cars back, follows him all the way east to Avenue A. At Tenth Street and Avenue A, McLain jumps out and slips into Tompkins Square Park, where he joins a bench full of homeless juicers, who razz him mercilessly about both the style and condition of his suit. Ignoring the soup kitchen sandwiches that lie beside them in plastic bags, the men pass a pint, and when it reaches McLain, he helps himself to such a long pull, their laughter turns into howls of protest.

Not for long, however, because as O'Hara watches from a nearby jungle gym, McLain pulls out his wallet and hands each man two bills; judging by the reaction, they're not singles. Then McLain gets up and displays the same largesse toward the occupants of the next bench and the one after that, duking every bum in sight like the Sinatra of Tompkins Park. Having done what he could for the standard of living in the southwest corner, McLain heads to the center of the park and slips bills to the owner of an elaborately loaded cart and two of his friends. His ill-gotten cash tapped out, McLain enters the dog run set aside for small dogs and sits on the bench in the corner. With all the yapping and commotion, it takes O'Hara several minutes to see that McLain is weeping.

26

Tuesday night O'Hara gets out of the subway again at Twenty-third and Eighth. Just as she did the previous night, she walks west toward the river until she is standing in front of the strip club, outside of which McLain went Beckham on the bouncer. The place is called Privilege, and O'Hara is quite sure the irony is unintended. It is housed in the ground floor of a boarded-up fleabag hotel, and its one flourish is the mane of teased-out hair drawn onto the back of the *P* on the awning. O'Hara pushes through a classy metal turnstile and enters a murky interior laid out like the rungs of hell. Room opens on room—a dancer and a pole at the center of each—culminating in a private chamber where select VIPs enjoy the privilege of getting dry humped and pickpocketed out of the cash they have left. And when the empty light goes off in their wallets, there's the ATM, the only link to the outside world, glowing in the corner. The setup's as cold as a heart attack, but at least the thermostat's pushed up. You can't send girls on stage with goose bumps bigger than their tits, and for the first time all day O'Hara isn't freezing. The other perk is the sound system, and the DJ knows exactly what he or she is doing. The Fiona Apple single "Criminal" revs up as O'Hara reaches the main bar. To a sampled beat, Apple boasts about being a bad, bad girl, and for all O'Hara knows it's true, but the little blond stripper lip-syncing the lyrics as she lazily sways her arms overhead is a lot more convincing. And when Justin Timberlake's "Cry Me a River" pours into the room, O'Hara almost forgets her feet are killing her. She sips her nine-dollar beer and looks around. Halfway down the bar, a grotesquely swollen face leans toward the straw sticking out of his Heineken. O'Hara walks over and extends her sympathies: "What the hell happened to you?"

"Motorcycle accident," says the man through a busted jaw.

"What was that?"

"Motorcycle accident," he repeats, eyes brimming with pain.

"You hit a snowplow? The only reason I ask is because it looks more like you got the shit kicked out of you." When this gets the gargoyle's full attention, O'Hara's flashes her shield. "I just want to know why the kid was here."

"Ask Sylvie," he says, and, trying very hard not to twist his neck, points over his shoulder with his thumb. "She's head mom. And please don't say nothing."

"Not good for the career?"

"No."

O'Hara pushes through a door marked EMPLOYEES ONLY. On the other side, half a dozen girls surround a space heater, their casual nakedness entirely different from the preening nakedness of the dancers on stage. Sylvie is the only clothed woman in the room, thankfully, because she's pushing seventy. "The little pimp wanted his girlfriend's back pay," says Sylvie. "I told him, she wants it so bad, she can come in herself." O'Hara takes out a picture. "Yeah, that's Holly. At least that's her dancing name, Holly Gomez. She worked Monday nights."

"Her real name was Francesca Pena. She was murdered a week ago."

"I thought she looked a little like Holly," says Sylvie. "No wonder she didn't show up."

Only Sylvie's advanced age keeps O'Hara from decking her on the spot. "It doesn't bother you that one of your dancers got murdered? And they call you 'head mom'?"

"I never get to know the girls," says Sylvie. "That's the only way to do this job."

When O'Hara leaves, the petite Hispanic dancer O'Hara noticed while talking to Sylvie takes the stage. Apparently, it didn't take long for Privilege to find a new Pena. She has the same sturdy legs and small top and the same short, dark hair, and when she recognizes O'Hara from the backroom, she flashes a dazzling smile. Before O'Hara can return it, the DJ cues up the Guns N' Roses ballad "November Rain" and the dancer spins away.

When the song was released as a single off *Use Your Illusion I*, O'Hara was twenty-one, fresh out of the Academy and working plainclothes in an Anti-Crime Unit in Times Square. That winter, it seemed like the video, the one that starts with Axl marrying Stephanie Seymour and ends with her funeral at the same church, was playing every time she turned on the TV.

As O'Hara pushes toward the bar, the girl smiles again and throws herself at the pole. When she lets go, her momentum sends her skipping toward O'Hara, who reaches up and slips a twenty into her g-string.

27

Bruno is fourteen pounds of empathy. He knows right away O'Hara is hung over and doesn't resist when she turns around and gingerly heads for home after five measly blocks. Safely back in the kitchen, O'Hara is about to call in sick again, when she sees that her own answering machine is lit up. In the ten minutes it took to walk Bruno, four new messages have come in. Hoping to Christ they have nothing to do with Axl, she hits PLAY: "Flumygoddammfuckingass!" shouts her sergeant, the angry words glommed together like congealed pasta. At least it's not Axl. Message two, ten seconds later: "I trusted you, O'Hara, and you fucked me without the Vaseline. Don't worry, I'll never make that mistake again." Despite her predicament and piercing headache, O'Hara smiles at the unintended ambiguity. Message three, seconds later: "Darlene, how you doing? Just did an all-nighter on a history paper and thought I'd catch you before you left for work." This time the caller is in fact her son, and although she's not sure she buys the part about the history paper, she is delighted by the sound of his voice. "Thanksgiving was a piece of cake," continues Axl on tape. "Both her 'rents are MDs and drive matching blue

Beemers, but all they wanted to hear about was my mom the New York City detective. It was like you were there. Love you. Hope you're good. So long for now." O'Hara smiles as long as it takes to cue up one last addendum from the sergeant: "If you're well enough to hang out at strip clubs, O'Hara, you're obviously well enough to work. I expect to see you at the start of your shift." Regarding Axl's call, O'Hara couldn't be much happier and is relieved he passed his first social test so handily. Regarding Callahan, she is more perplexed than alarmed. She hasn't told anyone about Pena and Privilege, except Krekorian. So how does her dumb-ass sergeant know about it?

The Wednesday-morning papers in their blue plastic sheath lie on the table where she dropped them. When she rips the bag open, the stripper's pole at Privilege is on the cover of the *Post*. Above it is the twenty-four-point headline BI-POLAR. MURDER VICTIM LED DOUBLE LIFE. The *Daily News* goes with AN ATH-LETE, A SCHOLAR AND A STRIPPER and Pena's innocent-looking headshot from her prep school yearbook. Even worse, Darlene O'Hara, NYPD detective, is in both stories. That shameless bitch Sylvie must have called the papers for the free publicity. No wonder she's still herding strippers in her golden years.

There's a second problem. O'Hara's car is on East Fifth Street. Her visit to Privilege had left a sour taste. To rinse it out, she stopped at her new favorite bar, Three of Cups, and when she stumbled onto the sidewalk after four Maker's Marks, was in no condition to drive. That means the subway. There's a delay on the 1 train, and O'Hara shows up forty-five minutes late for her own reaming. Not to mention badly hung over. In one way, however, the hangover is fortuitous. Without it, she'd never nail that hangdog expression of abject contrition.

Callahan blows hot about O'Hara's glaring lack of judgment, maturity, teamwork, the potential risk to herself and a high-profile case and most of all her blatant lack of respect for Callahan. But with nothing coming back from O'Hara, it's hard work. When Callahan says, "Let's make one thing real clear," she knows he's winding down. "Your participation in this investigation—officially, unofficially, on duty, off duty, is over. The case is with Homicide South now, where it belongs. You and Krekorian are back to precinct business. Understand? No more playing homicide detective. You've done enough harm already. That's it. We're finished."

It's as mild a rebuke as she could have hoped for, but those last couple of cracks are too condescending to leave alone. "I guess no one's going to congratulate me," she says.

"You listen to a word I said?" asks Callahan, disgusted.

O'Hara leaves Callahan's office and walks over to Krekorian, who's at his desk pretending to stare at his computer. "That was classic, Dar. You're literally halfway out the door, and you can't keep your mouth shut."

"Nope," says O'Hara, painfully aware that her one snide remark undid twenty minutes of semi-brilliant Method acting. And then in a whisper, "Come talk to McLain with me."

"Is that an intelligent thing to do right now?"

"Nope."

28

When O'Hara and Krekorian get to McLain's temporary new
home in Hell's Kitchen, McLain is vacuuming his host's living
room rug, and despite the beer in his hand, is doing a terrific
job.

"David," says O'Hara, "when were you going to tell me
Francesca danced at Privilege?"

"I wasn't," says McLain, and turns off the machine. "Her
stripping, which she did exactly once a week for four months,
has nothing to do with anything. It was easy, and it paid well.
End of story."

"That place is a magnet for assholes. One of them could
have killed Francesca. Maybe even the goon you beat the crap
out of."

"You were there? Next time, feel free to jump in."

"I was considering it, but it hardly seemed necessary. You
learn that at soccer practice?"

"No," says McLain with a sheepish smile. "A Jet Li video."

O'Hara and Krekorian leave McLain to his chores, but
not before O'Hara pries the can of Pabst from McLain's hand
and pours it down the sink, an egregious act of maternal

interference and wastefulness that elicits an arched eyebrow from her partner. "You're still sweating out last night's Maker's Mark," says Krekorian in the elevator, "and you confiscate a man's beer? He's vacuuming, not operating a forklift."

"That doesn't count as heavy machinery? I can't help it. The kid's loyalty gets to me. He doesn't mean a word of that crap about stripping being no big deal. Otherwise, he wouldn't have given away her wages like they were radioactive. Plus, he vacuums." O'Hara saw no reason to inform Krekorian that Pena's stripping money was actually removed from the bouncer's wallet and probably far exceeded anything owed to Pena.

"How about learning those moves from a kung fu flick?" asks Krekorian. "You buy that?"

"Not really. But he's obviously an athlete. You should see him ride a bike with no hands wearing a suit two sizes too small."

"What the fuck is that supposed to mean?"

O'Hara and Krekorian have just stepped back onto Ninth, when a call comes in for O'Hara from the *Post* reporter who filed this morning's story. Before she can stop herself, O'Hara is repeating the same far-fetched party line McLain fed her. "It's not enough for you guys that a teenage girl is raped, tortured and murdered; now you have to drag her name through the mud," she says. "It's an expensive town, and Pena needed the money. This has nothing to do with anything except selling papers."

"You don't think the fact that Pena worked as a stripper is news?"

"I don't. If I had the body for it and NYPD's blessing, I'd strip too. Why the hell not?" Krekorian taps O'Hara on the shoulder and pulls his finger briskly across his neck, and O'Hara finally hangs up. "Dar, you ever hear the expression 'no comment'?"

They stop for coffee and don't get back to 19½ Pitt for another forty minutes. When they do, Loomis and Navarro look at her anxiously as Callahan calls her back into his office. In a chair beside Callahan's desk is the commanding officer of the Seventh, Captain Aaron Hume. In front of it is Jeff deCastro, her delegate from the Detective Endowment Association. O'Hara knows deCastro wouldn't be here unless she's jammed up. Hume points at the chair beside deCastro. "Have a seat, O'Hara," he says. "We got a situation. Like everyone else here, I read all about your exploits at Privilege. Until I just spoke to your sergeant, I didn't know that you were out there on your own, having called in sick three days in a row. Callahan tells me he called you out on this matter less than two hours ago and made it abundantly clear that your involvement in this homicide investigation is over. Is that true, O'Hara?"

"Yes, it is."

"Then why the hell did I just get a call from that arrogant fuck Patrick Lowry at Homicide South, who tells me that one of their detectives just saw you and Krekorian walk in and out of a building on Ninth, where they happen to know McLain is staying? In other words, even though you had just been told to back the fuck off, you went directly from Callahan's office to talk to McLain. But that's not all, O'Hara, and again I got to hear it from Lowry. Two days ago, Lowry found out that McLain, who regardless of what you may think is our prime suspect in a high-profile murder, fired his assigned lawyer and hired another public defender, Jane Anne Murray, who we all know is a massive pain in the ass." *You mean she's a decent lawyer,* thinks O'Hara. "Lowry wondered what prompted the change, so he called Rikers and had them go through their log. It turns out that right before McLain called Murray, you visited him."

"But that's still not all," says Hume, a decent enough CO whom O'Hara had always gotten along with till now. "Ten minutes ago, Callahan gets a call from a *Post* reporter seeking comment for a story for tomorrow's paper. It's not set in stone yet, but the approximate headline is DETECTIVE ON MURDER CASE SEEKS PERMISSION TO STRIP. What the fuck is going on with you, O'Hara?"

"I never said that, captain."

"The reporter made it up?"

"Essentially."

Hume doesn't waste his breath on a lecture, just tells O'Hara to go home. "Pending a hearing in a couple weeks, you're suspended for a month. You're lucky I like you, O'Hara, or it would be three. Lock your piece up before you leave."

Stunned, O'Hara pulls herself out of the chair and walks out of Callahan's office. The detective room is dead silent, and if you saw the faces of the men on O'Hara's team, you'd think that what just happened to her had happened to them. O'Hara keeps a brave front, but inside she's sixteen again, leaving the office of the school nurse at Bay Ridge High after being required to pull her hippy blouse up over a nine-month bulge. She picks through the mess on her desk as if she's looking for something important but in fact is too rocked to think straight. In the midst of her pathetic pantomime she knocks her phone and it rings. She thinks her fumbling set it off, until it rings again. "Detective O'Hara," says the polished voice on the other end. "This is Richard Mayer. I'm an attorney calling on behalf of a client with information of value to your investigation." O'Hara first thinks it's a prank. One of the guys is trying to get a smile out of her. But everyone on her team is in the room, and none of them is on the phone. Mayer, who can't know she's just been suspended, must have gotten her name from the papers, and O'Hara knows she doesn't possess whatever poise or good judgment might be required not to take his call.

As everyone in the room stares at her, O'Hara gives Mayer her cell number and hustles him off the recorded line. After he hangs up, she says, "This isn't a good time, Mom. I promise, I'll call as soon as I get home." Then she turns to the room. "Moms," she says, "somehow they always know."

"Your mother doesn't have your cell number?" asks Loomis.

"Written it down twenty places and can't find any of them," says O'Hara.

"Really?" says Krekorian.

Although O'Hara's heart has been abruptly jolted to full speed, she feigns the depressed torpor she felt a minute before. Slowly and haphazardly, she gathers her coat and belongings and trudges out of the room. With the same underwater gait, she walks down the stairs and crosses the street to her car, where she stares up at the skinny window of the detective room and waits for her phone to ring.

29

The following evening, at ten minutes before midnight, O'Hara gets buzzed into a limestone town house on Forty-ninth just east of Third and rides an open cage elevator to the top. Richard Mayer, wearing a cashmere blazer and pressed old-guy jeans, waits in the barely lit marble foyer of the penthouse, and as he guides O'Hara through a series of just as dark rooms, she wonders if Mayer is going for atmosphere or saving on his Con Ed bill. Mayer leads O'Hara into a small den. There's just enough light for O'Hara to see that the man sunk in the corner of the couch, looking old, frail and busted, or roughly the opposite of how he looks on camera, is Henry Stubbs, coanchor of CBS's local evening news. "Detective," says Mayer. "This is Hank Stubbs."

"I see that," says O'Hara, as Stubbs sinks deeper into the furniture.

"The reason we're here," says Mayer, "is that eight months ago Hank went on a date with Francesca Pena arranged through an escort service called Aphrodite."

Mayer hands O'Hara an American Express receipt dated April 9, 2005, along with a stamped passport, airline tickets and a bill from the Convent Garden Hotel, all of which put Stubbs in London over the long Thanksgiving weekend that Pena was murdered. To call O'Hara a fan of Stubbs is an exaggeration, but he is certainly the only weekend anchor whose smarminess quotient is low enough for her to stomach, and sometimes she catches the show after Bruno's walk. She would have guessed forty-eight. The passport says sixty-one, and even in shadow, he looks all of it.

"Just one date?" O'Hara asks Stubbs.

"Correct," Mayer answers for him.

"You didn't like her?" asks O'Hara, this time twisting in her chair to face Stubbs front on.

"I liked her a lot," says Stubbs. "I asked for her again but was told she had left the agency."

"Three thousand dollars," says O'Hara, glancing at the Amex receipt. "What do you get for that?"

"Good question," says Stubbs, his anchorman baritone diminished beyond recognition.

"I mean, how much time?"

"Two hours."

"Fifteen hundred an hour, and you wanted an encore. Must have been pretty special."

Stubbs's attempt at a smile comes out a grimace.

"I think we've accomplished everything we can this evening, Detective," says Mayer, leaning forward and bringing his hands to the knees of his expensive jeans. "I don't have to remind you that my client has reached out voluntarily at enor-

mous personal risk. His information deserves to be treated
with the utmost discretion."

Puh-lease, thinks O'Hara. With Pena's stripping front-
page news, Mayer and Stubbs figure her call girl past can't be
far behind. This is nothing but a calculated gamble to save
Stubbs's high-paid celebrity gig. Under different circumstances, O'Hara would chew Mayer a new asshole on the spot,
but luckily for Mayer, discretion suits the suspended O'Hara
as much as Stubbs. "I appreciate that," she says.

An hour later, O'Hara is back downtown in the Seven, albeit
in a highly unfamiliar part, sharing a table with her partner
in the second-floor lounge of the recently opened Rivington
Hotel. The corner table looks out across Rivington at the an-
tique signage for Economy Candy. Below them, even at one in
the morning, the street is jammed, the only thing moving the
ratted-out bikes of the delivery guys, greasy takeout dangling
from the handlebars. The hotel lounge is exactly the kind of
high-end spot no self-respecting cop would ever set foot in,
which is why Krekorian chose it.

There don't seem to be any waitresses, so O'Hara gets up
and heads to the bar, passing a full-size pool table beneath an
elaborate plastic chandelier. Playing eight ball at dive bars is
one of O'Hara's preferred activities, so she can't help noticing
that the table is both empty and free, with no slots for quarters by the ball return. Then again there are no balls or cue
sticks either. Just as curious is the small library of books set

out for guests at the end of the bar. Weary travelers wanting to thumb through something while they drink have four titles from which to choose: *The Photography of Atget*, *The Earth Sculptures of Robert Smithson*, a memoir by Paul Bowles and a mini-biography of the emperor Hadrian. O'Hara hasn't heard of any of them, although God knows Lowry probably has: the only thing missing is a coffee-table book on the lost art of sutlery.

"Single malt," says O'Hara when she finally gets back to their table with the drinks. "We're drinking expensive tonight."

"Celebrating your suspension?"

"No, you coming here."

"Why you doing this, Dar? Everyone knows you're the best detective in the Seven. It's just a matter of time before you make grade."

"I think it's about the expression on Lowry's face."

"You're crazy."

"Borderline," says O'Hara, clinking his glass. "But you're not. And you came anyway. It means a lot."

"No thanks needed, Dar."

O'Hara tells her partner about the visit to Mayer's town house. "A stripper *and* a hooker," says K., nursing his aged scotch. "This girl must be your new hero."

"There are worse things a person can do."

"Saint Darlene O'Hara, patron saint of sex workers. I guess you want me to track down that credit card payment."

"That would be lovely, Serge." O'Hara glances back across the street at the sign for Economy Candy. It looks convincing, but for all she knows it could be a facade thrown up by developers to give hotel guests a more textured urban view, as purely decorative as the pool table nobody plays on and the books nobody reads. "So K., how the fuck do you even know about this place?"

"Everyone has a dark side, Dar."

"Oh, that's right, I remember. You went to college."

30

On a prime retail stretch of Ludlow, just south of Stanton, eeL displays a bicycle in the window. The small store, however, is not a bike shop, and except for that one prominently displayed BMX model, favored by twelve-year-olds in the projects and thirty-five-year-olds downtown, sells nothing else bike related.

Then again eeL sells very little of anything. As far as O'Hara can tell, its entire inventory is half a dozen T-shirts and sweatshirts, many adorned with the same camouflage pattern; two styles of jeans; and a shelf of Japanese fashion magazines. O'Hara has noticed other boutiques in the Seven selling merchandise just as piddling and random, but now that Krekorian has traced Stubbs's three-thousand-dollar credit card payment to here, O'Hara knows how at least one of them stays in business.

The owner of eeL is listed as Evelyn Lee, thirty-two, of State Street, Brooklyn, and an Asian woman of approximately that age sits behind the counter.

"Great stuff," says O'Hara after stretching out her perusal of the store as long as possible. "Beautifully edited."

"Thanks," says the woman, smiling over her laptop. "Let me know if you need any help."

"Actually," says O'Hara, "I'm looking for the owner: Evelyn Lee."

The mention of Lee, which occurs to O'Hara is eeL backward, erases the smile from the woman's face and sends her English into a nosedive. "She not here on Fridays," she says, snapping her Mac shut.

"Any idea when she will be?"

"Never here," says the woman, shaking her head discouragingly. "Sorry, English no good."

"But you can read this," says O'Hara, picking up the library copy of *Prep* lying open beside the register. "Impressive."

"Who you?"

"Who me? Me NYPD. Who you?" Rather than waiting for a reply, O'Hara reaches for the python slouch bag hanging from the back of the woman's chair, and removes the purse. "E. Lee," she reads off the license.

"Me Eva, not Evelyn. Lee common name in Korea."

"So I hear," says O'Hara, still staring at the license. "The Lee I'm looking for is also thirty-two and also lives on State Street, Brooklyn. Thanksgiving morning, a nineteen-year-old girl named Francesca Pena was murdered not far from here, and we know she worked for you because we've traced the money from one of her johns to this ridiculous store. You're in serious trouble, Evelyn, and not because you only sell six T-shirts. I suggest you start talking in complete sentences."

"Which client are you referring to?"

"You tell me."

"Francesca Pena worked for me for less than a week. And that was eight months ago. She went by Holly. Holly Gomez."

"How many times you send her out?"

"Three," says Lee. "One each with three different clients."

"Was there a problem?"

"On the contrary. Holly, apparently, was a natural. All three clients raved—five stars, standing ovation, two thumbs-up. They kept calling, asking for more dates and offering to up their fee, but Holly was in the wind. It cost me a lot of money and made me look like a schmuck."

"I need those names."

Lee hits a key on her laptop and glances at the screen. "April ninth was a TV news guy named Hank Stubbs. Maybe you've heard of him. The other two, on the tenth and eleventh, were just names and credit card numbers."

"I need what you have on all three."

"I'll give it to you right now," says Lee, not making even a feeble attempt to protect the privacy of her clients.

"I like new Evelyn much better," says O'Hara as Lee re-boots her Mac. "Where you from anyway?"

"Tenafly."

31

Monday morning, while Daniel Delfinger places his glasses on the corner of his leather-trimmed desk, sticks his head in his wastebasket and loses breakfast, O'Hara takes advantage of the unobstructed view of the back wall to learn what she can about the forty-three-year-old tax attorney and youngest partner of Kane, Lubell, Falco and Ritter. Behind wood and glass frames are a law degree from Harvard and a citation for making Law Review, a picture of his wife and three very young children in front of a looming suburban McMansion, and a sequence of photos of Delfinger and three old friends taken annually over some twenty-five years in the same spot in a Coney Island playground. Over the years, Delfinger morphs from a conspicuously overweight teen to a slim, nearly attractive adult, the only trace of his adolescent weight problem the chubbiness in his boyish cheeks.

The concise message, carefully laid out for easy absorption, is here is a kid from the neighborhood who worked hard and made good, yet hasn't forgotten where he came from. O'Hara's take is less generous: here is one more hypocrite and pig with more money than taste. But she does give him a couple of points for Coney Island and hanging on to old friends. "You going to be all right?" asks O'Hara.

"You tell me," says Delfinger, his voice echoing in the chrome receptacle and male-pattern baldness shining through his Jewfro. When he stops puking long enough for O'Hara to show him a picture of Pena, Delfinger readily concedes the tryst, which he says was arranged through Aphrodite eight months before. "It was April eleventh. I remember because it was the day my partners and I settled a large malpractice suit. But she didn't use Francesca. It was less ethnic, Maggie or Molly."

"How about Holly?"

"Could be."

"You didn't want another date?"

"No."

"Daniel?"

"Fine, I tried to arrange another. Several times. But she was gone, quit the business, whatever. Hard as it may be to believe, I moved on."

"Where were you the night before Thanksgiving?"

"Home."

"In that?" asks O'Hara, pointing to the wall.

"In Stamford, Connecticut. Our office closed early. I got home about two and was there all weekend."

"Can anyone verify that?"

"About twenty people. Wednesday till Saturday we had my wife's parents, her two sisters, their husbands and their seven kids."

"That's thirteen."

"Eighteen including us."

"Your wife will confirm that?"

"Depends how you ask. Be nice if you could do it in a way that doesn't ruin my life. I got the number for Aphrodite out of the back of *New York* magazine. How illegal is that?"

"I wouldn't worry. Wives in big houses have a way of getting over stuff."

"Naomi hasn't gotten over anything in five years," says Delfinger, staring back down at the wastebasket like he's about to pay it another visit.

"Nothing else proves you were home?"

"My secretary has my calendar. It shows the last hour I billed Wednesday and my first one Monday."

"You got to do better than that."

"I should have an on-line E-ZPass statement, if I haven't tossed it already."

No pun intended, thinks O'Hara. "Let's see it."

Still green, Delfinger finds his November statement among his recently deleted mail and prints it out. O'Hara sees that Delfinger enters and exits Manhattan through the same West Side toll plaza as O'Hara. Southbound, he always clocks in close to 7:00 a.m., and northbound never before 6:00 or after 8:00, except on Friday when it's never later than 4:00 p.m. Wednesday, he headed home at 1:20 p.m., and the next hit on his account is the following Monday at 6:58 a.m.

"Let me ask you something," says O'Hara, nodding at the wall. "Why are you working here? No offense, but this place doesn't look like Harvard Law School."

"That's what I like about it. At the white-glove firms, I'd be the designated Jew. Or even worse, have to act like I wasn't one at all—join a country club, pretend my parents are from Connecticut. I came here instead, work with people I actually like and made partner in six years."

"Not to mention a shitload of money."

"I'm well compensated." Delfinger may be a scumbag, but based on the rank smell seeping out of his wastebasket, O'Hara can't believe he has the stomach to torture someone to death. Besides, everything he told her matches with what she's already heard from Stubbs and Lee. "Take some of that money and buy your wife something very very expensive," suggests O'Hara, and when she slips the statement in her coat and pushes away from the desk, Delfinger is so grateful she hasn't called his wife, he looks like he could cry. Instead, he opens a small lacquer box and hands her his card. "Ever need help on your taxes, it's on me."

32

The picture O'Hara drops on Juergen Muster's gray enamel worktable draws a blank but not a denial. "Aphrodite is far and away my favorite service in the city," he says, running his long fingers through his short professionally tousled light brown hair. "Evelyn sends me three or four girls a week, and usually they do me right here in this office. It clears my mind, helps me concentrate."

Wonderful, thinks O'Hara.

And then raising his voice to throw it over a translucent partition just behind him, Muster says, "Isn't that so, Christina?"

Last night, when O'Hara Googled Muster, his name popped up all over the place: perfume bottles, nightclub VIP rooms, magazine makeovers, even that topless Kate Moss billboard for Calvin Klein looking down over Lafayette and Houston. One gushing profile dubbed him downtown's most inspired design polymath. *More like Polly wants a hooker*, thinks O'Hara, which is surprising in a way, since Muster, long and angular, as if he sketched himself, with chiseled features covered with three days of silvery stubble, is certainly attractive enough not to have to pay for female attention.

"Try concentrating on this," says O'Hara, pointing at the picture. Other than the picture, the only item on Muster's pristine oblong table is a sketch pad open to a blank page. When O'Hara slides the photo toward him, Muster's pale green eyes follow its progress like a spreading stain.

"Lee said you called her repeatedly. Said you practically begged for a second date."

"Holly," says Muster. "Yes, of course. The picture doesn't do her justice."

"How'd you feel when Lee couldn't contact her?"

"Chagrined," says Muster, whose beautifully cut gray suit makes it hard to tell where his desk ends and he begins. "One thing about having sex with pros, as opposed to quote unquote amateurs, is that I generally get to decide when the relationship is over. Getting dumped by a call girl is quite deflating."

"Your feelings were hurt?"

"Something like that. But I didn't fly into a murderous rage. And if you check with Evelyn, you'll find I've been on many other satisfactory dates since."

Delfinger's office was a photo album. Muster's Tribeca loft is uncluttered by evidence of anything as corny as a family or a past, and every detail is pared to within an inch of its life. How disappointed Muster would be, thinks O'Hara, if he knew that when it came to women, he had the identical taste as a slimmed-down striver from Brooklyn, who buys his suits off the rack and drives home to the suburbs every night. *Men spend their whole lives propping up a personality a millimeter thick.*

"Where were you at four a.m. Thanksgiving morning? And please, for their sake, don't tell me with your family."

"Right here," says Muster. "The same place I was last night and the night before that. I do have a mother and father, by the way, but they're in Vienna; we don't celebrate Thanksgiving on the Danube."

"What were you working on?"

"A spoon."

"Really, sounds like an important project."

"The right spoon can change the world."

"Anyone with you?"

"Christina."

Without a word, O'Hara gets up and crosses to the much smaller space on the far side of the partition, where a painfully thin Asian woman looks up from her large coffee. "I hope he pays well," says O'Hara.

"He doesn't."

"So?"

"He's brilliant, and believe it or not, I'm learning something. If I hold out a little longer, I can work in any design studio in the world. If I quit, I'll have eaten ten months of shit for nothing."

"The night before Thanksgiving, you were here with him all night?"

"Pathetic, isn't it?"

"You don't have family either?"

"In LA. I couldn't afford to go back anyway."

"Any proof that you were here?"

"Why would I lie for that cretin?"

"Same reason you won't quit. Would you blow him too if he asked—you know, to clear his mind?"

"None of your business."

"Probably not," says O'Hara, leaving a copy of Pena's picture and her card. "But a young woman your boss had sex with got murdered. You think of anything, please give me a call."

As anxious as O'Hara is to leave this pristine loft and get back on a filthy New York City curb, she stops in Muster's office on the way out. "On your date with Holly," asks O'Hara, "was there any role play?"

"She dressed like a schoolgirl," says Muster. "Plaid skirt, button-down white shirt, long wool socks. Even had a book-bag and Partridge Family lunchbox. It's all in the details, and hers were excellent."

"Your idea?"

"No. All I ever ask for is a nice ass and no tits."

"But you liked it, the little girl routine?"

"It's a hopeless cliché. But it worked for me."

33

O'Hara picked the Empire Diner because it's just up the street from Privilege. She hadn't been there for a couple of years and had forgotten just how swank and sophisticated it is, not to mention how gay. An enormous bald-headed black man sashays over and introduces himself as Maître Dee Dee. As he walks her to her table, O'Hara is reacquainted with the warm candle-light bouncing between the black countertops and the mirrored ceiling, and the dude playing Gershwin on the upright in the corner, and the small backlit bar dispensing old-timey cock-tails. Monday night's special is "the painkiller"—rum, cream of coconut and pineapple juice—but O'Hara restrains herself. She orders an Amstel and watches the cabs race up Tenth.

Erika, who goes on at midnight, arrives first. When O'Hara slipped that twenty in Erika's g-string, O'Hara's NYPD card was tucked inside. Erika helped O'Hara get in touch with Teresa, Leslie and Ina, and they walk in together ten minutes later.

"Well, look what the cat dragged in," says Dee Dee, es-corting them over. "You ladies are so gorgeous, you must be celebrities."

"Try strippers," says the six-foot blond Teresa.

"For real?" says Dee Dee, putting his hand to his mouth. "You are my heroes and role models. I'm a drag queen—Monday nights, Bar Dot."

"I learned half my act from drag queens," says Ina when Dee Dee departs. "The less you got, the harder you work it."

"Tell me about it," says Erika.

O'Hara is buying. She, Teresa and Leslie order burgers, Erika a niçoise salad, and Ina, French toast. "What do you remember about Holly?" asks O'Hara after the food and cocktails arrive.

"Not much," says Leslie. "She stuck to herself."

"That's a nice way of putting it."

"That stuck-up Ivy League bitch wanted nothing to do with any of us," says Teresa, and takes an enormous bite of her burger. "Acted like she was the only stripper in the history of the world who'd ever read a book."

"Does *Harry Potter* count?" asks Erika.

"It better," says Leslie. "I'll say one thing—the bitch could dance. She did stuff on the pole I'd bust my head trying. And growing out her bush like she did. She was crazy."

"Crazy smart," says Teresa. "It made her stand out."

"She ever do a little schoolgirl routine?" asks O'Hara.

"Shit, we've all done that."

"We've never ridden out on stage on a tricycle," says Leslie, laughing.

"It was a Big Wheel," says Erika. "And that was sick."

"About how much could she make a night?" asks O'Hara.

"Not much," says Teresa. "All she did was the stage."

"To make money," explains Erika, "you got to do lap dances. Holly didn't go back there. If she was lucky, eighty dollars a night."

After the girls leave, O'Hara calls Krekorian, who is just ending his shift. "Serge, I need another favor. You got to go to Privilege for me."

"But they've got girls on stage, Dar. And they're practically nude." O'Hara explains that she needs to find out if Pena had any stalkers or obsessive fans. "How am I going to find out that?"

"They got a little office in the back. If you go through the credit card receipts for Monday nights, maybe the same names will keep showing up. I'd do it, but I can't risk ending up in the *Post* again. I'll be waiting up the street at the Empire Diner."

O'Hara moves to the counter and settles in near the little altar of a bar, where she orders a martini. The more she thinks about what the girls told her, the less it adds up. If Pena wasn't willing to do lap dances, she could do better as a waitress. And if she had some kind of academic fascination with strippers, she'd be talking to them and taking notes instead of snubbing them. Or maybe Pena was just a dilettante scratching an itch, dabbling on the wild side, like with those three dates through Aphrodite?

Krekorian walks in just after four in the morning, as the place is filling with x'd-out club kids. "T and A makes me thirsty," he says. "I need a beer."

"Hell with that," says O'Hara, nodding toward Dee Dee. "This guy makes a great martini, and you're having one."

"Sure he's a guy?"

"Technically, he's got to be."

"Why's that?"

"He's a drag queen."

Dee Dee assembles and dispenses the cocktail with precise flair, and as O'Hara watches her partner unwind in the candlelight she wonders why the two of them never hooked up. Probably because they like each other too much and don't want to blow it.

"You're right as usual, Dar. Dee Dee makes a hell of a martini."

"Was I right about anything else?"

"As a matter of fact, you were. The Holly Gomez Fan Club had two charter members. On the last ten Mondays she worked, one showed up eight times, and the other didn't miss a night. And both were women."

"They have names?"

"Two old friends of yours: Deirdre Tomlinson and Madame Evelyn Lee."

34

O'Hara looks down at the uneven surface of her kitchen table. When she dragged it home from the yard sale last summer, it seemed like a miraculous find. Now, with a certainty that applies to nothing else, she sees that it's a couple of inches too big for the space and a wobbly piece of crap.

At Empire, O'Hara was on her best behavior, stretching three martinis across four hours, but when she got home K.'s discovery left her too amped to sleep. She fixed herself a nightcap and another, and kept pouring until her supply of Maker's Mark was gone. She didn't get out of bed until three in the afternoon. Now it's five, and except for the unsought realization about her kitchen table, she would be hard-pressed to say how the last two hours have passed. O'Hara refills her mug at the stove and tries again to focus on the unlikely pair of strip club regulars, but her clumsy brain stumbles from question to question like someone bumping into furniture in the dark. When O'Hara tries to imagine the scene at Privilege, it always comes out like slapstick, the two women falling off their pink Naugahyde stools as they clamor for Pena's/Holly's attention.

Did the two sit near each other or at opposite ends of the

horseshoe bar? Is it possible they weren't aware of each other? After so many overlapping Monday nights, that seems unlikely, but did Tomlinson know that the Jappy Korean with stylish bangs is a madam? And did Lee know that her painfully thin rival is an associate provost at NYU? Did they take turns lobbying the scholar athlete, or was it strictly a bidding war, the two seeing who could stuff more twenties into Pena's stretched-out g-string? Wouldn't that make a lovely picture for the NYU yearbook.

O'Hara knows that for both women, landing Pena was a major coup. NYU and Tomlinson beat out every top college in the country, and in a city that never sleeps, Lee outrecruited as many escort services. At the memorial, Tomlinson claimed she'd called Pena so often because she had a terrible if vague feeling Pena had fallen in with the wrong crowd. Clearly, it was more than a hunch, but maybe she was essentially telling the truth, and she and Lee were playing the parts of good and bad angels, Tomlinson showing up every week to try to shame Pena back into her clothes and school and Lee trying to lure one of her best potential earners deeper into the sex trade.

After a while, the surplus of scenarios hurts her head as much as last night's drinking. O'Hara looks up from her table at the printout of Pena's tattoo, which is stuck to her freezer with a magnet from Riverdale Pizza, although calling that pizza is a bit of a stretch. That dollar sign at the center of the heart creeps her out as usual, but the *T*, *B* and *D* on the left, and *H*, *T* and *B* on the right mean no more than ever, and neither Tomlinson's initials nor Lee's fall neatly out of the letters. At seven, O'Hara feeds Bruno his dinner and leashes him for his walk, and on the way back stops at her car for the plastic bag of fan mail she took from Pena's locker. She rereads the first note, then spreads the other four over her wobbly kitchen table.

2. I miss you. Pizzas and my bed are too big when you're gone.

3. No one will ever touch you the way I do.

4. I miss you so much, I can taste it.

5. What's the matter, F? I thought you liked the way my tongue felt inside you.

Although the notes are undated, O'Hara rearranges them in what she believes is the order in which they were sent. In the new sequence the sign-offs start with "sincerely," "affectionately" and "ardently Tommy" and escalate to "achingly" and "desperately Tommy."

Sincerely, affectionately, ardently Tommy. Touching, licking, tasting. Tommy. O'Hara thinks of the pinball-playing Tommy from the rock opera, and when it hits her, it's so obvious, she feels like the deaf, dumb and blind one. Tommy is not a horny nineteen-year-old boy, but a horny thirty-something assistant provost. "Tommy" is short for Tomlinson, the nickname she reserves for lovers or at least the most special of college applicants.

Forget good and bad angels, thinks O'Hara. Maybe this whole thing is personal and romantic, two thirty-something women fighting over a teenage girl. One woman, Lee, wins, and the other, Tomlinson, despite all her education and culture, and the priceless art on her wall, turns out to be a very poor loser. Just another downtown lesbian love triangle gone bad.

At nine-thirty at night, O'Hara's head and stomach still feel like crap, and the surge of adrenaline brought on by her belated discovery makes both feel worse. Unfortunately, O'Hara doesn't have it in her to sit back and wait till morning. On the off chance Tomlinson is working late, O'Hara calls her office and hangs up when she gets her machine. As she expects, Tomlinson's home number is unlisted, but ex-detective Larry Elkin at Campus Security is happy to provide it.

"While I got you," says O'Hara, "is there anything you can tell me about Tomlinson? Her personal life, her professional life, rumors, anything?"

"We both got to NYU about the same time," says Elkin, "but I've only met her once. I'm pretty certain she resides on the Isle of Lesbos, but so do half the faculty. No student, as far as I know, has filed a complaint, not that I would know necessarily. About three years ago, we dispatched an ambulance to her apartment. An overdose, accidental according to her. I guess that means she changed her mind."

Thirty seconds later, much too soon to have thought it through, O'Hara, her head and heart pounding, has Tomlinson on the phone. "I need to talk to you about Francesca."

"Can't it wait till morning?"

"No, it can't."

"It's ten o'clock, Detective. I'm about to go to sleep. Can you at least tell me what this is about?"

O'Hara hesitates, but whether owing to Tomlinson's lying

to her from the beginning, racial stuff she is barely aware of, or the lingering effect of too much gin and bourbon, she can't resist rattling Tomlinson's cage. "It's about Privilege," says O'Hara. "Not the concept . . . the one on Twenty-third, with a capital *P*, and a big mane of hair sticking out the back." When the phone falls silent, O'Hara regrets it immediately.

"Meet me in front of the library in half an hour," says Tomlinson.

"I'm coming from Riverdale. Can we make it an hour?"

"You were the one in such a hurry, Detective. Half an hour or I'm gone. And good luck finding me."

35

Wincing at the light and siren pulsing from her dash, O'Hara races onto the West Side Highway and pushes her straining Jetta through southbound traffic. Condos and crumbling piers pass in an eighty-mile-an-hour blur before she swoops down past the Hustler strip club warehouse and the *Intrepid*, a carwash and Circle Line. She exits at Fourteenth and runs reds from the meatpacking district to Fifth, then south to Washington Square, where she double-parks just east of the library.

Lights still flashing, she jumps out of the car and checks her phone, which she trusts more than her watch: 10:27. She got downtown in twenty-three minutes. Across the street students file in and out of the huge Starbucks. O'Hara could use some coffee, too, but waits on the curb and tries to concentrate on what she'll do when Tomlinson arrives. Where would be a good place for them to talk? What questions should O'Hara open with? She can't afford to repeat the same mistake she made on the phone and show her hand too quickly.

Six minutes later, Tomlinson still hasn't shown. Maybe, as Elkin said, she changed her mind. More likely she just took off. O'Hara leaves a message on Tomlinson's home voice mail, waits three more anxious minutes, and at 10:36 pushes through the revolving doors into the Bobst Library. Inside, the towering atrium is filled with a voluminous hush. Clicking heels, the whir of a waxing machine and the tinkling of voices are buried beneath fourteen stories of empty air.

On the far side of the atrium, an elevator opens with a ping. A female Asian student wearing fashionable leather boots— two-thirds of NYU's students seem to be Asian girls—steps onto the checkered black-and-white floor of what must be the grandest ballroom in the city south of Grand Central. With the unself-conscious exhaustion that envelops everyone still in the building at this hour, the girl starts out across the gleaming tiles, and in anticipation of showing them to the guard at the door, pulls two books from her backpack. To her right, at the long checkout counter, three students stand sleepily in line.

"Detective," a female voice calls out from the top of the atrium, "up here." The Asian student stops in her tracks, looks up and screams as O'Hara, who has already pushed through the turnstile, cranes her neck towards the ceiling. She does it just in time to see a small figure on the highest balcony climb from a chair to the top of the Plexiglas barricade and hurl herself out over the atrium. The body, which O'Hara knows is Tomlinson, hits the polished tiles no more than ten feet west of the girl.

For a certain interval, the imploding pulpy splat of that horrible mismatch stuns the smaller scattered sounds into silence. The Asian girl screams again and collapses, and the sound of her books and bag hitting the floor reverberates through the room. Then all hell breaks loose: multiple alarms sound, security guards race toward the girl and Tomlinson, and from the sides and the balconies the shrieks of onlookers join the din. Two maintenance workers sprint toward Tomlinson and cast a not quite big enough tarp over her crumpled body and the crimson background flowering beneath it. Amid the screams and scrambling and alarms, O'Hara slips back out through the turnstile and revolving doors.

36

Outside is a riot of emergency response—ambulances, squad cars and NYU rent-a-cops converging on the southeast corner of Washington Square. O'Hara walks to her car, flicks off the light flashing on her dashboard and pulls away from the curb. She takes Mercer across Houston and after several tight cobblestone blocks, pulls over and turns off the lights.

O'Hara knows that the emptiness of the library will work against her because it will sharpen the focus of the handful of witnesses. Of the small number of maintenance workers, security guards and students in the building, at least one will have heard Tomlinson call out to her before she jumped. And even if O'Hara is wrong about that, detectives will soon discover that Tomlinson received a phone call from O'Hara thirty-six minutes before she jumped, and more than likely O'Hara's hasty exit from Bobst will be captured on video. Lowry and Grimes could be knocking on her door in Riverdale in a couple of hours.

To get her brain to slow down enough to think, O'Hara leaves her car and walks the dark streets in a four-block square. She keeps her eyes trained on the greasy cobblestones for rats, but only encounters European tourists strolling arm in arm. As she inhales the cold air and stuffs the panic back in its box, she gazes at the well-dressed men and women, their faces flushed from after-dinner drinks.

Back in her car, O'Hara calls Lee. At this point, Lee is all O'Hara has left, and even that won't be for long. Once O'Hara's role in tonight's catastrophe hits the airwaves, whatever leverage O'Hara has over Lee will evaporate. Lee answers on the first ring, and her bright solicitous tone is encouraging. It indicates she's still hoping to cooperate her way out of trouble.

"Evelyn," says O'Hara with all the casualness she can muster, "have Stubbs, Muster and Delfinger gone out with any of your other girls?"

"Off the top of my head, I can tell you Muster has for sure. Hang on a second, and I'll check the others. . . . The answer is yes. In fact, I've got an Irish girl named Molly who went out with all three. Pick a spot, and I'll have her meet you there in an hour."

When Lee hangs up, O'Hara cracks her window and calls Mary Kelly, her third-floor neighbor, who has a key to her place. O'Hara doesn't worry about calling this late because the eighty-five-year-old widow hasn't slept two hours in a row in years.

"Of course I'll take in old Bruns," says Kelly. "Me and Mister B will have a grand old time."

"Not too grand, Mary. The last time you took him he turned his nose up at kibble for a month. And no beer in his water bowl. I'm serious."

"Don't be a worrywart, Darlene. It's not becoming."

At one in the morning, as promised, a very pretty brunette sticks her head into the Rivington Hotel's second-floor lounge and strides confidently toward O'Hara's corner table. She has the same petite frame as Pena and, dressed in the latest, darkest denim and a vintage shearling coat, looks as chic as any of the hotel's guests. "Lovely choice," says Molly with a generous dollop of brogue. "Best of all, I've never worked here."

"When Lee said Irish," says O'Hara, "I thought she meant Brooklyn Irish like me."

"Not a genuine mick from Killarney."

"Bay Ridge more likely."

"Well, I've been here three years now. I'd take the accent with a grain of salt if I were you."

O'Hara orders a couple of Irish whiskeys and asks Molly what she remembers about Stubbs, Delfinger and Muster.

"Muster is a proper shit. Quite gorgeous, though, with his bespoke suits and shirts and every hair carefully out of place. Never been to his apartment. I used to straddle him in his office on his midcentury modern desk chair, while he chatted with clients on speakerphone, and his assistant worked next door, completely aware of what was going on, which was half the point, I take it. Until he was done, which was quite quickly, he barely acknowledged I was there, then pointed to a beautiful envelope on the corner of his desk. Elegant handwriting, I'll say that, particularly for a man."

"And Delfinger?"

"Very different, but worse in a way. Acting all guilty and

neurotic and Woody Allen about what was going on. Do it or don't, but spare us the drama, thank you."

"And how about everyone's favorite anchorman, Hank Stubbs?"

"He did have quite an anchor actually."

"Really, it's not a myth?"

"What they say about TV newsreaders? Absolutely not. But I felt quite badly for Mr. Stubbs. He may be the loneliest person I've ever met. For someone in my business, that's saying something."

"Anything scary about any of them?"

"Not really. They were more scared of me. That's almost always the case."

Molly's observations ring true, but O'Hara is less interested in the johns than in Lee. "Lee told me that Pena went out once with all three men and then disappeared," says O'Hara. "Do you think Lee suspected that Pena had taken her clients private?"

"Three dates and out, wouldn't you? Poaching, we call it."

"Was Lee concerned about poaching?"

"Massively. Do you know how Pena's body was mutilated?"

"Why?"

"Right after I joined Aphrodite, Lee sent me a loathsome picture of a girl she claimed to have caught poaching."

"Still have it?"

"No, but I'll never forget it. It was of a white girl, early twenties, and someone had gone to work on her face with a box cutter. There was cuts from her forehead to her chin and hundreds of black stitches to close them. Amazing she didn't bleed to death. And in the center of it all, her dead, drugged-out eyes. It was highly effective. Any temptation I might have had for cutting out Miss Lee was gone forever."

The Rivington Hotel is only three blocks from eeL. At two in the morning, the metal grate is down and Lee's number gets a recording: "Congratulations. You're either very smart or very lucky because you've found your way to Aphrodite, the city's most discriminating service for the most discriminating tastes." O'Hara grabs a lid off a nearby garbage can and walks back to the storefront. She clangs it against the grating, until Lee, wearing a headset, pulls it up over the window and opens the front door.

"What did Molly tell you?"

Ignoring her, O'Hara pulls down the grate and shoves Lee into the tiny office at the back of the store.

"Close that," says O'Hara, pointing to her computer.

"What is it? What did she say?"

"Was Pena poaching?"

"Poaching?"

O'Hara opens her coat so Lee can see the handle of her gun.

"No. She wasn't."

"Then what were you doing at Privilege?"

"Trying to get her to come back."

"By stalking her? Bullshit."

"Look, maybe she was poaching," says Lee, scared. "How could I know for sure?"

"You ever threaten your girls about poaching?"

"No."

"You don't send them a photograph of a disfigured girl?"

Lee's face takes on a strange expression, and her head collapses into her hands. "You want to see the picture, I'll show it to you. I need to turn the computer back on."

Soon the picture Molly described so accurately fills the screen of Lee's laptop. The girl's face was even more carved up than Pena's.

"Was this it?" asks Lee. As O'Hara nods yes, her stomach turns. "So this really scared Molly? I'm amazed."

As O'Hara looks over her shoulder, Lee scrolls to the top of the page and stops on the name of the Web site: rickyshalloweenmakeup.com.

37

"Turkey on a Kaiser roll," says O'Hara. The swarthy, hollow-eyed man behind the counter listens with the kind of tender smile found at that hour only on someone who reached adulthood in another country. While he assembles her sandwich, O'Hara surveys the refrigerated offerings in the rear, which include a shelf packed with yellow-, lime- and coral-colored waters named "serenity," "recovery" and "energy." After the night's debacles, O'Hara could use vats of all three but opts instead for a six-pack of amber-tinted stress water called Amstel Light. At the counter, she adds two large coffees, then lugs her 3:00 a.m. supper to the car. She eats in the passenger seat with the window rolled down. The sandwich, cold air and coffees will help keep her working. The beers are for later to sleep.

Where she will happen to sleep remains to be decided. Although she would never admit it, the Rivington Hotel is growing on her rapidly. She tries to rationalize this choice by telling herself the how safe it is, since the odds of anyone looking for her there are pretty much zero. Unfortunately, so is the chance of her being able to afford it, but she calls anyway out of morbid curiosity. "Our junior suite starts at $515 a night," says a man, who otherwise sounds quite reasonable. "That's a little more than I wanted to spend," says O'Hara, before washing down the last of her sandwich with a gulp of burned coffee. "I could talk to my manager. Perhaps, we could do a bit better. It is three in the morning, after all."

"Please don't bother."

O'Hara remembers Hotel Suites on Rivington, but she also remembers the aroma of breakfast curry in the manager's office. Then thankfully she recalls the anomalous little Howard Johnson's a couple of blocks north on Houston. She parks the Jetta on a Fifth Street block reserved for cops working out of the Nine, figuring that no one in that precinct would recognize her car and no one else would look for it on a street lined with police cars. At 4:15, she signs for a room at the Howard Johnson Express Inn ($180 a night) and ten minutes later, lets herself into a freezing third-floor double. The room reeks of stale smoke. She has traded the smell of curry for cigarettes.

With Tomlinson dead, and Lee a dead end, O'Hara is essentially starting over. And her case file is on her kitchen table back in Riverdale. All she has to generate new leads is her memory, a six-pack and the rapidly diminishing effect of two large coffees. For a couple of minutes she leans against the brown headboard, sick with panic. Then she gets up and moves to the desk, slides open the drawer and pulls out the single complimentary piece of hotel stationery and the skinny white HoJo's pen, and begins to put together a timeline of Pena's last day. Working slowly and steadily, she fills the page with eight entries, each surrounded by an inch or so of empty space.

1. 6:00 p.m. to 8:30 p.m.: Pena with McLain at 78 Orchard Street.

2. 8:30 p.m.: P. leaves the apartment.

3. 10:21 p.m.: P. uses her Amex card to buy two CDs at Tower Records at the corner of Broadway and Fourth.

4. 10:30 p.m.: P. meets Chestnut, Case and Singh on Rivington, between Bowery and Chrystie.

5. 2:30 a.m.: Chestnut, Case and Singh leave.

6. 3:30 a.m.: P. leaves alone, walking east on Rivington. Ten feet north of the corner of Chrystie and Rivington, P. is struck from behind and dragged into the Atelier construction site. For approximately ninety minutes, she is tortured and raped. Estimated time of death—5:10 a.m.

7. 6:00 a.m. (approx.): P.'s body, wrapped in two shower curtains, is dragged out of the building, loaded into a vehicle and dumped in East River Park.

8. 11/28/05—12:45 a.m.: P.'s body is found in the park in a closed-down men's bathroom.

As burned out as O'Hara is by her endless night, it takes her more than half an hour to create the timeline. When she's done, she takes it, along with her six-pack, and stretches out on the bed, where she reads through it slowly again and again. On the fourth reading, she stops at the sixth entry and underlines the phrase "Ten feet north." Exhaustion, aided by beers one through five, has shrunk the space between her eyelids to a slit. Before they close entirely, she jots "one hour and fifty-one minutes" at the bottom of the page. Then she drains her last beer and carefully places it back in the carton with the other empties.

38

Wednesday at eight in the morning, jackhammers start breaking up pavement on Houston. *Jesus Fucking Christ.* O'Hara throws on her coat, takes the back stairs down to the lobby and steps into the flat December light. Directly next door to the Howard Johnson Express Inn is a modest storefront bearing the hand-lettered sign YONAH SCHIMMEL'S KNISH BAKERY—ORIGINAL SINCE 1910, and when O'Hara sees the squad car rolling toward her up Houston, she decides that's original enough for her. In her five years in the Seven, O'Hara has had the pastrami and brisket at Katz and bagels and lox from Russ and Daughters, but never darkened the threshold of Yonah's, and as she steps through the door, a tray of the eponymous steaming cylinders ascends from the basement oven via a creaking dumbwaiter. O'Hara orders one and a coffee, and in a move that surprises the ancient blond at the register, who doesn't take O'Hara for a tourist, she drops another fourteen dollars for one of the black Yonah Schimmel Original Knishes T-shirts hanging from a piece of twine stretched across the ceiling.

Back in her room, O'Hara's first encounter with Jewish comfort food is highly satisfactory. For a potato-eating mick, it's hardly a stretch. The surge of well-being induced by the warm, sweet starch recalls the unlikely optimism she felt just before she passed out. The last thing she did the previous night was read the timeline, and after a quick search of the room, she picks it up off the floor, where it had fallen behind the desk.

She scans the eight entries and stops on the underlined phrase, "Ten feet north." It refers to the spot where Narin, the crime scene tech, found several thick drops of Pena's blood on the curb and sewer drain. According to Narin, this is where Pena was struck from behind, probably as she bent over and got sick, but why had she turned north before she was attacked? Pena's apartment at 78 Orchard was only a seven-minute walk from Freemans, but had she been heading home, she would have walked east straight across Rivington Park, not turned north. And if Pena was not going home at four in the morning, where was she headed? Even in the harsh light of a sober morning, it's a promising question. Unfortunately, at least for now, O'Hara has no way of answering it.

O'Hara's final note, scribbled at the bottom of the page, is "one hour and fifty-one minutes." That's the time between when Pena left McLain at her apartment and her next known destination, when she purchased those two CDs at Tower Records. Three weeks after Pena's murder, those one hundred and eleven minutes have still not been accounted for. What makes that gap in the timeline such a promising area of investigation is that Pena lied about the time twice, first to McLain when she told him she was meeting her friends for dinner, then to her friends when she told them she had just come from the gym.

O'Hara gets up from the desk, and for first time since she checked in, opens the curtains. The third-floor room faces west over Rivington Park, and standing close to the window and tilting her head to the south, she can see the outline of the Atelier towering over its tenement neighbors on the far side. Its steel skeleton looks like an ink drawing. At the base of the construction site, O'Hara can just make out the spot where Pena was attacked.

While O'Hara gazes over the leafless trees, a crosstown bus hisses to a stop beneath her. In front of the glass shelter, at the corner of Forsyth and Houston, is a vending machine for the *Post*. SHE JUMPS is the headline in the window, and as intended, it gets O'Hara to race down and buy a copy. It isn't until she's back in her room that she finds the sidebar on page 11 headlined COPS ANXIOUS TO QUESTION DETECTIVE WHO FLED THE SCENE. Illustrating the story are a pair of video stills of a woman who looks a lot like O'Hara pushing in and out of the revolving doors of Bobst Library.

The pictures are too small and blurry to cause any problems with good Samaritans on the street, but obviously Lowry and Callahan and everyone else in the Seven know who it is. This is confirmed by the six new messages on her home answering machine: four from Callahan, one from Lowry and one from a detective she's never heard of, who's working the Tomlinson suicide. O'Hara deletes the messages and tosses out the paper. At this point, the only thing that can save her ass is finding Pena's murderer. Thinking about anything else is a waste of brain cells.

O'Hara showers, pulls on her new black T-shirt. It's a little tight, but at least it's clean, and, sinking her chin into the collar of her parka, she steps back into the raw morning. She passes her favorite knishery and the Sunshine Cinema, turns right on Eldridge and east again on Rivington. Directly across the street from the Rivington Hotel, she steps down into a basement-level vintage clothing store called Edith Machinist.

O'Hara has been aware of this place, like HoJo's and Yonah's, for years but never come close to walking in, and has never bought a "vintage" or, as she would describe it, a used piece of clothing in her life. As with Schimmel's, however, she sparks immediately to the displayed items, their unique character and uncrass beauty, and she can see the affection that went into every choice. The bags hanging from pegs on the side wall look like the portraits of a dozen singular women and the boots arranged in a half circle on the floor up front like the class of whatever huddled for a reunion photo. O'Hara slips off her parka and tries on a big-buttoned navy peacoat. The dark blue sets off her fair skin and still-wet hair, and the snug fit looks so stylish that the haughty salesgirl, who had written off O'Hara with one look at her rubber-soled shoes, abandons her breakfast to help.

"That looks great on you," she says. "And your T-shirt is so cute I can barely stand it." Mixing and matching from three different decades, she finds O'Hara a gray cashmere sweater with black stripes, a braided leather belt with circular brass buckles, and to be worn with her jeans stuck into them, a pair of oxblood Bally boots. To cover her telltale red hair and freck-

les, O'Hara tops the ensemble with a blue Nordic ski cap and
big fat Gucci shades. Total cost: $290. Upgrade in her style
quotient: priceless.

By the time O'Hara steps back onto the street, she looks so
chic she can barely recognize herself, let alone be mistaken for
a cop. With her old clothes dangling from her arm in two crisp
bags, she blends right in with the skinny shopping machines
walking in and out of the Rivington Hotel or sitting in the
window at Moby's little tea shop. Although her new look at-
tracts little extra attention from male pedestrians, her female
rivals are all over it, icily checking her out from cap to boots.

Feeling conspicuous yet invisible, O'Hara walks down Orchard until she's facing the street from Pena's old stoop. If she's
going to be able to fill in those missing one hundred and eleven
minutes, O'Hara needs to retrace Pena's steps after she left her
apartment for the last time. Since left leads south toward Chinatown, and Pena's next known stop, Tower Records, is north
of Houston, O'Hara starts with the calculated guess that Pena
began by turning north up Orchard. If O'Hara is correct, she
should be able to prove it, even nineteen days later. Almost
every shop on the street has a video camera mounted above the
door, and a few of them probably even work.

After coming up empty at a bookstore, whose prominently
displayed camera is a fake, and a bodega, whose tapes only go
a couple of days back, O'Hara tries her luck at Joe's Drapery, a
substantial enterprise occupying a large building at the southeast corner of Orchard and Delancey. When a salesman with a

bad rug hurries over, O'Hara fends him off with her shield and explains what she's after.

"Then you want Seth, our head of security," says the man with a wink. "Seth wears many hats. The one he likes best is heir apparent."

He directs her to a basement office, where a twenty-some-thing slacker with impeccable bed head sits on a ratty couch, amusing himself on his cell. Mounted to a wall above him are two TV monitors, each split into quadrants displaying the feed from the store's eight video cameras.

O'Hara introduces herself as a detective and points to the live view of Orchard in the upper-right corner, which captures pedestrians as they stroll north and south. "You still have the tape from that camera from the night before Thanksgiving? That would be the twenty-third."

"We should. We try to hold them twenty-one days before we start to tape over." The kid points to a cardboard box in the corner. "Knock yourself out."

"Or," says O'Hara, after sniffing the air like a narc, "you could get off your spoiled ass and help me out."

"That sounds like a much better idea." He jumps off the couch, pulls what he estimates is the right tape from the box and stuffs it into the player. As it spools backward toward the center of the tape, pedestrians lurch past the store on a sun-filled afternoon, and when he hits PLAY, they stride more gracefully in the opposite direction. Then he hits PAUSE and reads the time code in the upper-right corner: 11:23:13:07.

"You got the right day," says O'Hara. "Now fast-forward to eight-twenty p.m."

He does, but the tape runs out at 18:42, almost two hours short, and when he pops in the next one and reads the time code, it's the following day.

"Jesus Christ," says O'Hara, "you're taping over it now."

Seth hurries to the two four-deck recorders in the corner, ejects a tape, and, looking apprehensively at O'Hara, pops it into his player and spins forward until today's overcast morning turns abruptly into the night of November 23. The time code reads 11:23:19:27.

"No sweat," says O'Hara. "We made it with an hour to spare."

Seth speeds forward to 20:20 and hits PLAY.

In the right corner of the screen, chilled New Yorkers pass the store's Orchard Street entrance. After so much fast-forwarding and rewinding, seeing them move in real time is like watching grass grow, at least until the time code hits 20:38, and Francesca Pena rushes into view.

"Stop," says O'Hara. "Rewind a little, stop, and play it again." Pena reappears in the frame in her dark red jacket, her hands in her pockets and body tilted forward into the wind. With her short back hair and delicate face, she looks a little like Audrey Hepburn. "That girl is hot," says Seth.

"She's dead," says O'Hara, seeing her alive for the first time.

Seth replays the tape three more times. From the way Pena carries herself and braces against the cold, O'Hara believes that Pena has started out on a journey of some distance, and is not just walking a couple of blocks. She also surmises that Pena is running late.

"So what are you going to do when you take over, Seth?" asks O'Hara, already moving toward the stairs.

"What do you think I'm going to do? I'm going to liqui-date—make a deal with a developer and turn the building into condos."

"Dumb question."

Over the next couple hours, O'Hara works slowly north up Orchard on both sides of the block. When a squad car carrying Chamberlain and another rookie patrolman, Ivan Rodriguez, rolls slowly by, they stare right through her. From Delancey to Rivington, and Rivington to Stanton, she doesn't get a thing, but from Stanton to Houston, she gets three new hits. The first is on a camera attached to a bridal shop called Adrienne's, the next two at American Apparel, a big new clothing store at the corner of Orchard and Houston, whose gleaming white walls are covered with soft-porn photos of its wholesome girl-next-door employees. On the first camera, Pena is still truck-ing north at the same determined clip. On the second camera, she has turned west on Houston, and the third, mounted on the westernmost corner of American Apparel, catches Pena step-ping off the curb and heading west across Allen. Pena steps out of frame halfway across the wide double block. O'Hara hustles out of the store and finds the spot where Pena stepped off the curb. Her line across Allen heads directly to the entrance of the Second Avenue subway station.

39

When O'Hara runs down the steps and sees the size of the station, whose walkways and platforms disappear into the distance in every direction, her heart sinks. Back in her motel room, with her feet finally out of those frigging Italian boots and thawing on the electric radiator, she can think more clearly. People entering the Second Avenue station can take the F or V train south to Borough Hall and Brooklyn or north to Thirty-fourth Street, Rockefeller Center and Queens. Since Pena just spent ten minutes walking north, the uptown option seems more likely. Pre-9/11, finding footage of Pena anywhere in the subway system would have been a logistical nightmare, if not impossible. Now at least there's one central location, in the transit police precinct under Union Square, where detectives can review film from every camera in the subway system, but under the circumstances, O'Hara can't risk going there herself.

"Dar, you're out of control," says Krekorian when she gets him on her cell. "Callahan and Lowry are already up my ass."

"I'm sorry about that, K., but I'm in too far. I stop now, my career is over."

"Yeah, well, whose fault is that?"

"I'm a fuckup, Serge. Always have been."

"Utter bullshit."

"But here's the thing. I'm making progress. That last night after Pena left McLain at her apartment, I got her entering the Second Avenue subway station on Allen at 8:43 p.m. Almost certainly heading uptown."

"How the fuck you get that?"

"When she left her apartment, she had to go somewhere. I guessed north, and got her on four different cameras. The last one has her heading straight toward the subway."

"Why do you think that's so valuable?"

"A couple reasons, but mainly because it's all I got."

"That must have been quite a sight at the library last night."

"The sound was worse."

"Good acoustics in there?"

"The best. But as disturbed as Tomlinson must have been, I don't see an eighty-eight-pound anorexic breaking into a construction site, dragging Pena in and out, and loading her on and off a van."

"So you want me to find out where Pena got off the subway?"

"I need it, K. It's my only chance."

"Calm down, Dar. My shift doesn't start till four. I'll go to surveillance now. No one has to know I'm doing it for you."

"And if they find out?"

"I go to business school, make more money than my brother."

"Then he'll punch you."

"That will be the day."

"Listen . . . ," says O'Hara, but Krekorian, who senses that his partner's gratitude and stress are pushing her dangerously close to tears, cuts her off. "It's going to take me a couple hours at least. I'll call you from there. And I'd stay off the street as much as possible. Lowry has warrants out on you—one for interfering with an investigation and leaving the scene of a crime."

"Fuck him."

"That's how I feel."

40

Over the next couple of hours, O'Hara becomes highly knowl-edgeable about the layout and contents of a double room at the Howard Johnson's Express Inn at 135 East Houston Street. She straightens the bed and hangs up her new old clothes, throws away the wrappers from breakfast and rinses her Amstel emp-ties like they're family heirlooms. She calls down to the front desk and puts two more nights on her credit card and kills close to ten minutes washing her underwear in the sink and drying it with the tiny theft-proof hairdryer.

When she can't hold off any longer, she picks up the remote and turns on the TV. Judges Alex and Judy and the C-tier talk show hosts squeeze entertainment out of people's tawdry little fuckups, and the soaps are like porn without sex. Her one great piece of luck is that her room is too dowscale to have a minibar. Overcoming the urge to head to the corner for another six-pack is hard enough.

Somehow, she gets through the two hours and ten minutes before Krekorian calls back.

"Sounds like you're watching TV too," says Krekorian. "Oprah?"

"I'd cut off a big toe for Oprah," says O'Hara. "She doesn't come on till four."

"Dar, we got Pena getting off the 1 train at 168th and Broadway at 9:06 p.m. And she's running."

O'Hara clicks off the TV and stares at the blank screen. Moreal and Consuela Entonces, the two girls from Pena's Big Sister program, live three blocks from that stop. Tida Entonces, their ex–junkie mom, told O'Hara that because of Thanksgiving, Pena didn't make her usual weekly visit and hadn't been there since the previous Saturday. So now there are at least three lies about those missing one hundred and eleven minutes.

"Dar, you there?"

"Just trying to think. Serge, remember the girls in the program I told you about? They live on 170th and Fort Washington Avenue. Stay at that same station and switch over to the cameras on the downtown side. Let's see if Pena gets back on that train."

O'Hara stays on the phone and hears a rush of tape, then a click when Krekorian says, "Stop."

"You're right on again, Dar. At 9:14, we got her coming back in on the downtown side, and both girls are with her, one in each hand. That's six blocks round-trip, plus in and out of the building, in eight minutes. I know the girl was a runner, but that's Olympic-level hustling."

"K., I'm heading uptown to talk to Tida Entonces. You call me the second you find out where they get off."

O'Hara runs the two blocks to Allen and hurries down the

same stairs Pena did fifteen days ago. After ten minutes on the empty platform, she catches an F train to Thirty-fourth Street, runs the block to Penn Station, and after another excruciating platform wait, boards an uptown A train. O'Hara is the only passenger in the car, and as the rattling local lurches through almost twenty stops, O'Hara thinks about Pena and her two young charges sprinting through the night. Where were they running to? Or what were they running from? At the deep 168th Street station, one of four elevators slowly carries O'Hara toward the surface. On the street, O'Hara tries to quicken the pace but her vintage boots don't do her any favors. By the time she covers the short distance to 251 Fort Washington Avenue, her T-shirt is soaked.

O'Hara checks her cell—still no call from K.—and waits for her heart rate to come down. She has barely thought out her approach to talking to Entonces, but with two warrants out for her arrest and cops cruising the neighborhood, she can't hang out on the street. When a tenant steps out of the locked vestibule, O'Hara spins and slips through the door.

On six, sour cooking smells fill the hallway. O'Hara tries to buy a little time by the elevator, but a dog goes ape shit from behind a chipped door, and an old crone, carrying her trash to the incinerator chute, eyes her suspiciously. Just like with Tomlinson, everything is moving much too fast. But she can't loiter in the hallway any longer. She walks down the blackened tiles toward 6E.

On the other side of the door, Entonces shuffles toward her in her house slippers. O'Hara hears the metal cover slip off the eyehole. The door opens and catches hard at the end of its six-inch chain.

"I barely recognized you," says Entonces. "You look different."

"Tida, can I please come in?"

"It's not a good time, Detective. The girls are home sick. You should've called first."

"Please, Tida. There's something we need to talk about. It's important."

Entonces unlatches the chain, and O'Hara follows her down the dreary hall. The new Justin Timberlake's coming from behind the door of the first bedroom, and girls' voices rise over it.

"The girls don't sound too sick, Tida," says O'Hara.

"What can I tell you? They fooled me."

They stop at the kitchen, spotless as ever, even with the girls home for the afternoon. Entonces nods toward the Formica table. "Have a seat. I just made coffee."

"Thanks. A glass of water would be better."

O'Hara drinks half of it in one gulp, as Entonces watches warily.

"Tida, why'd you lie to me?"

"What are you talking about?"

"You told me Francesca didn't visit the girls Thanksgiving week, hadn't been here since the previous Saturday. I just found out that's not true. She was here the night she was murdered. Wasn't she?"

Entonces's face crumbles. On a good day, Entonces is still an attractive woman. At least you can see the parts that were, but when she cries, all that time on the streets pushes through the cracks. From across the table, O'Hara watches Entonces age twenty years.

"I didn't want to lie about the girls going out with Francesca Wednesday night," says Entonces, "but I had to. The rules say Francesca can only take them out on weekends. To Children's Services, a Wednesday is always a weekday, no exceptions. Children's Services, they don't play. They'll use anything to take my girls away, even if it's dirty dishes in the sink. To them, I'm a two-time loser who never deserved my girls back in the first place."

Tida Entonces's explanation is not implausible, and she's right about Children's Services. A sniff of trouble and they'll snatch Moreal and Consuela back in a second. Entonces sobs softly, and O'Hara feels her own grip slipping too. Is she so hard up for a break in this case that she's grasping at straws, taking a couple of snatches of MTA video and blowing them up into more than they are?

"Detective, you don't look so good. You need more water?"

"Please," says O'Hara, and after Entonces refills her glass, takes another long gulp. "What did they do that night, Francesca and the girls?"

"Francesca took them out for a quick dinner," says Entonces. "It was her Thanksgiving treat."

"Where, Tida? Where did they go?"

O'Hara struggles to steady herself, as she runs the times through her head. They don't add up. At 9:14 Pena and the girls get on the subway, and barely an hour later, Pena is buying

CDs one hundred seventy blocks away. Where's the time for dinner? Before Entonces can answer, Consuela, the younger of her two daughters, wanders into the kitchen.

"I'm talking to the detective, baby," says Entonces.

"I'm thirsty," whines Consuela. She ignores her mother and opens the fridge.

"Then take your drink and let us be."

On the shelf at the bottom of the door is a carton of strawberry Nesquik. Consuela reaches for it, and her sweatshirt rides up on her skinny back, uncovering black markings surrounded by red skin. Squinting, O'Hara makes out the shape of a heart and a dollar sign at the center, and before she can stop herself, jumps up from the table and grabs the girl's thin wrist much too hard. Startled, Consuela drops her carton, and the pink-colored milk spills onto the kitchen floor.

"Consuela," says O'Hara, the kitchen spinning around her. "When did you get that tattoo?"

"Momma," cries Consuela, "that hurts."

"Get your hands off my daughter," screams Entonces. She is already out of her chair and rushing toward them. "Who the hell do you think you are?"

"I'm sorry," says O'Hara. "I didn't mean to frighten Consuela. But I need to know where she got that tattoo."

"You don't need to know shit. Get out of here this minute. Or I'm calling the police."

41

O'Hara pushes back out through the vestibule, to the curb, where a wash of milky light is all that's left of the day. Fort Washington Avenue is filled with the braying of just released Dominican and Puerto Rican schoolkids, one of whom careens through the clogged sidewalks on a small black bike just like the model in the window of Evelyn Lee's boutique. Still unsteady on her feet, O'Hara makes her way through the chest-high crowd, attracting hard stares from the more precocious preteens. The nascent street toughs are more adept at making a cop than Rodriguez and Chamberlain.

O'Hara buys a bottle of water and takes it to an island bench in the center of Broadway, rush-hour traffic whipping by in both directions. She's got a new message from Krekorian on her cell, and pressing the phone tight to her ear can just make it out. "Dar, spent two more hours in the MTA but never saw Pena and the girls get off. According to the tech, 103rd, Fiftieth and Christopher Street all have multiple cameras out, and there are so many holes in the coverage, they could have slipped through almost anywhere. I'd stay longer, but some of us still work for a living. Please call me before you do anything else ridiculous."

Too late for that, thinks O'Hara, but doesn't beat herself up with her usual brio. She shouldn't have grabbed Consuela, but spotting her tattoo more than makes up for it because it proves her instincts about the tattoo were right, and Lowry's were wrong. Whatever the reason, Consuela has the same heart-shaped pattern inked on her lower back as Francesca. And Consuela's tattoo was still fresh, the skin around it raw and pink. It couldn't be more than a couple of weeks old.

O'Hara extricates herself from the middle of upper Broadway and descends into the subway. On uptown trains, commuters are pressed up against the windows like aquarium guppies, while the southbound trains are empty. By 6:30, she is back on Houston, and just like on Fort Washington Avenue, she's the oldest human being in sight, not that that matters to the red-eyed counterman at her adopted bodega.

"Turkey on a Kaiser roll," he says with a smile. "Lettuce, tomato, little butter, little mustard?"

"Nobody likes a showoff," says O'Hara as she heads to the refrigerators.

Safely back in room 303, O'Hara cracks an Amstel and stares across the dark park. Uptown, she can follow Bowery all the way to St. Marks, each tenement topped with a distinctly different water tank. *Wherever you land*, thinks O'Hara, *the city absorbs you like a sponge*. In less than twenty-four hours, O'Hara has a new subway stop, bodega, sandwich order and view. The only thing missing is Bruno farting on the bed.

O'Hara unwraps her provisions on the desk. As she eats, she adds what she's learned to her timeline:

8:43 (approx.), writes O'Hara, Pena enters the Second Avenue
subway station at Allen Street.

9:06 p.m., Pena gets off the I train at 168th and Broadway. She's running.

9:14 p.m., Pena, with Moreal and Consuela Entonces, reenters 186th,
southbound.

Thirty-one of the missing one hundred and eleven minutes are now accounted for, and with a little more time to
consider it, Tida's story about Pena taking her girls out for
a quick pre-Thanksgiving meal seems like one more piece of
bullshit. If Pena and the girls got back on the subway at 9:14
p.m. and sixty-seven minutes later, Pena was at Tower Records, there's barely time to eat three slices of pizza and send
the girls home in a cab. Why would Pena run all the way
uptown for that? That brings it to four lies about this brief
stretch of time.

O'Hara deserves to enjoy her sandwich, and she does, along
with a second beer. Then she pulls out her cell and scrolls
through her received calls until she finds the one she got from
Lebowitz that evening while she was going door-to-door on
Rivington. The call came in on his cell, and when she calls the
number, he picks up on the first ring.

"Darlene, I've been worried about you."

"I messed up, didn't I?"

"Only if you believe what they write in the papers."

"In this case, I'm afraid, it's pretty much true."

"Then I'm sure you had your reasons."

"I like to think so."

"Pena?"

"Yeah. That's why I'm calling. At least something related to her. Did you work on the Tomlinson suicide?"

"Terri handled that one. But since as I had a personal interest in the case, I looked over her shoulder as much as I could get away with."

"Did Tomlinson have any tattoos?"

"No. Why?"

"I just found out that one of the girls Pena was mentoring had the same tattoo as Pena, same spot and everything. I wondered if Tomlinson did too. Some kind of secret sorority."

"No tattoos. I'm sure. And there's something else. I read through her blood work. She had fatal amounts of three antidepressants in her system, plus twenty milligrams of lorazepam. If she hadn't gotten to a hospital within the hour, Tomlinson would have died whether she jumped or not. I thought you might want to know that."

"I appreciate that, Sam," O'Hara says, and realizes she doesn't want the conversation to end. "I really do."

"Where are you staying?" asks Lebowitz.

"This boutique hotel on Houston you've never heard of. It's called Howard Johnson's. Very exclusive, very obscure. Not everyone gets the irony."

The joke falls flat and is followed by an awkward silence.

"That's funny," says Lebowitz finally.

"You sure?"

"You must think I'm a fatal nerd."

"I don't. Really. I mean I doubt it's fatal. Of course you know a lot more about causes of death than I do."

"That's funny too," says Lebowitz, and this time emits a sound very much like laughter. "It's good to hear your voice, Darlene. Please call again if you need anything else."

"It's good to hear your voice too," says O'Hara, and feels herself smile at Lebowitz's shyness as she hangs up.

The conversation takes O'Hara back to Bobst Library, not a place she wants to go. Once again she sees Tomlinson's skinny arms and legs windmill through the air, an image she had somehow managed to avoid all day. O'Hara pushes her attention from Tomlinson to her rival, Evelyn Lee. Maybe in O'Hara's embarrassment about that staged picture on the Halloween Web site, she wrote off the Tenafly madam too quickly. Lee might not be much of a pimp or a businesswoman, but that doesn't mean Pena wasn't poaching. And if Pena had taken one of Lee's clients private, then at least one of those johns, all of whom swore to O'Hara that they had never seen Holly again after their first magical date, was lying.

O'Hara looks inside the desk drawer for a second piece of HoJo stationery, but the cheap bastards only give you one. So she turns the timeline over, divides the back of page into three columns—one for Stubbs, Delfinger and Muster—and writes everything she can recall about those three interviews. When she's done, the only one O'Hara feels comfortable ruling out is Stubbs. Although, in retrospect, there's something off-putting about the way Mayer had all the paperwork waiting for her so nice and neat, and someone with halfway decent Photoshop skills could probably have forged them all, Stubbs's alibi still feels solid. She can't see Mayer risking that town house or anything else for a client, and besides, Stubbs was the only one of the three who came to her. Coming forward makes sense as a gamble to save a career. It doesn't make sense if you killed someone.

The other two alibis, however, are paper thin, and O'Hara is disgusted with herself for having accepted them so readily. Beacuse O'Hara was convinced Delfinger couldn't be the killer, she let him slide on a calender and an E-ZPass statement, and the only thing propping up Muster's alibi is a highly dependent subordinate who desperately needs the job. As O'Hara tries to add to her memory of those last two interviews, the phone rings.

It's not her phone. It's the hotel's, and against her better judgment, she picks up. "Someone's on his way to your room," says the overnight man at the front desk. O'Hara looks at her watch: 12:15. It's got to be Krekorian, just released from his four-to-midnight. But the footsteps in the hall are too light for Krekorian, and the knock on the door too tentative for a cop. O'Hara looks through the peephole, and she sees the dark, unruly hair of Sam Lebowitz. She can't see his face because he's staring at the carpet. Thrilled to see him and anxious to put him out of his misery, she pulls him into the room and kisses him on the mouth. Then she runs her tongue across his ear. "I've been wanting to do that for a while."

"Really?"

"Yup."

O'Hara hands Lebowitz an Amstel and jumps into the shower, washing her hair with the tiny bottle of shampoo on the ledge, and when she steps out of the bathroom her wet red hair and freckled thighs bracket a black Yonah Schimmel Original Knishes T-shirt. Gazing up at her, Lebowitz's face registers a level of excitement several times higher than anything he had experienced in his first thirty-two years.

"You drank all that by yourself?" asks O'Hara, pointing at the minuscule space at the top of his beer.

"It's the curse of sobriety," says Lebowitz. "My family has suffered from it for generations."

"Not mine," says O'Hara.

O'Hara pulls Lebowitz out of his chair and starts kissing him in earnest, and as she pulls off his shirt and unbuttons his jeans, sees something in his eyes and posture so immutably seventeen, she knows already she will never tire of fucking him.

"Sam, I got to say, you look even better without your clothes."

"In high school, I was getting picked on a little. My old man bought me a set of weights."

"That's not what I meant, Sam."

42

On Thursday morning Muster's Amazonian receptionist unlocks the oxidized steel door, and O'Hara, knish and coffee in hand, follows her into the fascistically minimal waiting area. O'Hara is desecrating an art object table with her breakfast grease when Muster arrives for work in a six-thousand-dollar bespoke suit and three-dollar Canal Street sneakers.

"What happened to you?" he asks. "*Queer Eye?* You look fabulous."

O'Hara flips him the bird, with Brooklyn nonchalance, and leaves it flapping in the breeze until Muster keeps stepping. A couple of minutes later, Christina trudges through the door. O'Hara follows her to her cube, where she collapses in her Aeron and lays her head on her desk.

"Remind me one more time," says O'Hara, "why you're working for this asshole."

"I've got very little experience and not much work of my own to show. If Juergen wants me to pick up his lunch and listen to him getting blown, and apparently he does, my choices are to deal or crawl back to my parents in Los Angeles. Believe me, I'm not doing that."

"See, that's why I'm here. Without you, Muster has no alibi. Considering everything he's holding over you, can I really believe you two were here all night?"

"Yes."

"Why?"

"Every girl draws the line somewhere. I draw mine between having to listen to someone cum and providing them with a phony murder alibi."

Instead of a cube, Naomi Delfinger is sequestered in a ten-thousand-square-foot postmodern in a leafy neighborhood in Stamford, Connecticut. It's on a private cul-de-sac where every third house is a teardown, the original fifties-era homes razed to make way for bloated suburban palaces. The new ones, like Delfinger's, tower above the tree line, as naked and out-of-scale as the Atelier.

Unlike her house, Naomi Delfinger is homely in a modest way. She is petite, small boned and plain, with faded brown hair and oversized tenebrous eyes. After O'Hara tells her she's an NYPD detective investigating a murder, Delfinger walks her through a two-story entrance decorated with studio portraits of her three daughters, and brings her into a huge kitchen with two of everything—ovens, dishwashers and refrigerators. They sit at a sunlit table looking out on a tarp-covered pool.

"Your girls are precious," says O'Hara.

"They were such a gift, particularly at my age."

Delfinger, who looks to be in her early forties, pours coffee and puts out cookies, which despite the double set of appliances, look and taste as if they're missing several crucial ingredients. "My husband told me about your visit," says Delfinger, and O'Hara tries to conceal her disappointment.

"Not many husbands would."

"Daniel said she was an exceptional young woman with a bright future. He told me you spoke to everyone at his office."

"Did your husband say what Pena did for the firm?"

"He said she was an intern and that she had planned to apply to law school in the fall."

"She was a call girl, Mrs. Delfinger. Your husband met her through an escort service called Aphrodite."

Since her first glimpse of Delfinger's wife, dwarfed by her immense front door, O'Hara saw her as a woman hanging by a thread and prescribed pharmaceuticals. Now Naomi Delfinger's eyes harden with resolve. "You drove all the way out here to tell me this? Is this how you get your kicks? If not, I don't see the point, because other than making me very unhappy, it doesn't change a thing. It certainly doesn't change the fact that my husband got home early Wednesday afternoon and didn't leave the house all weekend."

"When did he arrive?"

"About two. But I'm sure he told you that already."

"Was there anyone here other than you who can confirm that?"

"No, only my husband and me."

"No houseguests?"

"It was just the five of us, and quite wonderful," says Delfinger, enunciating each syllable with painful precision.

"Daniel is a very hard worker. Having him home five days in a row is a rare treat."

I bet it is, thinks O'Hara. "Your husband told me the place was packed with relatives—your parents, your sisters, their husbands and children."

"Detective, I'm going to have to ask you to leave."

Being kicked out of kitchens by lying women is getting tiresome. To buy a little time, O'Hara sips her coffee and reaches for another tasteless cookie. A photograph of Delfinger, the chubby teen in that Coney Island playground morphed into a patriarchal dweeb, smiles at her from one of the refrigerators, three young daughters in his arms. *Only the rich and the poor still breed this indiscriminately*, thinks O'Hara. The oldest looks four, tops, the youngest about a year, and the way everyone is bundled up against the cold, the shot had to have been taken recently. O'Hara looks at the smallest child again and estimates her age between eight and ten months. If it's the smaller number, she must have been born close to the date Delfinger met Pena.

"Your youngest looks like a real firecracker," says O'Hara. "I'm guessing an Aries."

"Very good, Detective," says Delfinger. "And according to anyone who knows anything about astrology, Tovah is the classic Aries, through and through."

Naomi Delfinger smiles, in spite of herself.

"Mrs. Delfinger, would you like to hear the date of your husband and Pena's tryst?"

"What I'd like is for you to leave. I've asked once politely. Now I'm asking again. Please."

"April eleventh," says O'Hara. Delfinger's face freezes, as if she's just been struck. O'Hara keeps talking, anything to stay in the room a little longer. "When I had my son, I didn't even know who I was yet. I was barely sixteen. I got kicked out of high school and was branded a fool and a slut, the perfect combination. It was quite the little scandal, even in Brooklyn."

"You have no reason to remember this," says Delfinger, "but April eleventh was a gorgeous spring day. New York Hospital had given us the loveliest hospital room I've ever seen. It looked straight over the East River. And Tovah was so easy, nothing like the first two. Dr. Shwab said 'push,' and out she came, as if she couldn't wait another second. My goodness, what a precious little girl. Daniel was so happy and proud. But of course he had to go back to work. At least that's what he said. The next day he gave me a ring from Tiffany's. Pena must have been his gift to himself."

"Me, it took thirty-six hours to squeeze out Axl. I haven't worked that hard since, and don't plan to. That's right, getting knocked up wasn't the only harebrained thing I did. I also named the kid Axl, after the singer for Guns N' Roses, who turned out to be such a knucklehead. If I wasn't going to name him something reasonable like Matt or Joe, I could at least have gone with Slash.

"People said I should put him up for adoption. It's not like I couldn't see their point. I was sixteen and running wild, going out and getting boxed every night, and in the nine months since I missed my period, I'd barely given the gink a single thought. I wore big blouses and put it out of my mind, pretended it wasn't happening. Like they say, denial is not just a river in Egypt. But when the time came, I found out giving away my kid was not something I could do. Surprised me as much as anyone else."

Delfinger shakes her head as if she knows where this is going and it doesn't apply. O'Hara keeps right on talking. "I'm not saying I'm a hero. To be totally honest, my mother raised Axl far more than I did. The point I'm trying to make is that you think you can't get through something, and it turns out you can. In fact, it can be a blessing."

Naomi shakes her head again, but much more feebly. To O'Hara, it looks like she's disintegrating.

"Axl got me kicked out of high school, disgraced my family and got all my girlfriends on the pill. He was also the best thing that ever happened to me. Maybe the only really good thing."

"That not what I mean," says Delfinger, staring at her hands. "I mean, no, Daniel didn't come home Wednesday night. Wednesdays he works late, stays in the city and rents a room at the Harvard Club. I assumed the night before Thanksgiving would be an exception, but I was wrong. He called that afternoon and said that if he didn't stay late, he'd have to work the weekend, then called again about eleven p.m. and said he was too tired to drive. He didn't get here until Thursday morning. You want another nice detail that says a lot about my devoted, sentimental husband? Guess what room he rents at the

Harvard Club—411. I thought it was because it was Tovah's birthday. Detective, I have three kids under the age of four, I'm forty-one and never had a job. What am I going to do?"

It's midafternoon when O'Hara backs out of the driveway and maneuvers through the obstacle course of bumps and gates that keep drivers to the posted fifteen miles an hour. Once past the white gates and sentry box, she finds a classic rock station playing ZZ Top and Alice Cooper. She cranks it full blast and sings along, shouting out the choruses as if her life depends on it. When that station turns to shit, she finds one just as good at the other end of the dial and sings along to vintage Mary J. Blige until tears stream down her face.

In the city, she parks near the Ninth Precinct again on Fifth Street, and although it feels disloyal to her overworked counterman, detours to a Polish diner on Avenue A for beef stroganoff over egg noodles. For dessert, she has a couple drafts at the dive bar next door.

Back in 303, she's calmed down enough to leave a long exhilarated and largely coherent message on Krekorian's cell. She catches him up on Consuela's tattoo and her visit to suburbia and the admission by Delfinger's wife that her husband was lying and never came home the night of the murder. "It was one lie after another from that cheeky fuck. He said the house was full of relatives, total bullshit. And after his whole little charade about tossing his online E-ZPass statement and then magically finding it in his recently deleted mail, it turns out he drove all the way up to Riverdale and went through the toll just to cover his tracks, then turned around and came back downtown on Broadway to avoid the toll. I swear to Christ, K., I'm so close I can taste it."

O'Hara hangs up, and she feels the full weight of the exhaustion she's held off for days. Without pulling the covers, she stretches out on the HoJo's bedspread. When the phone rings five hours later, she's shivering and the sky in the window is black. It takes several rings for O'Hara to realize she's not at home in Riverdale.

"Dar," says Krekorian. "I got bad news. They just found McLain's van in long-term parking at Newark Airport, and the mattress in the back is covered with Pena's blood. Lowry is on his way to Orchard Street right now to arrest him."

43

O'Hara's silence worries Krekorian. "Lowry had a whole department working for him," he says. "You had me." When O'Hara still doesn't respond, he adds, "I'll go to bat for you with the review board. Every guy in the Seven will. What room are you in?"

"303."

"Promise me you won't go anywhere. I'll come over as soon my shift ends. "

"I can't believe I lost to that blowhard fuck."

"You're lucky you didn't have to watch him parade around here with a stogie in his mouth," says Krekorian, relieved O'Hara has finally said something. "The guy thinks he's Bill Parcells."

"Close but no cigar. That's me in a nutshell." She wonders if some people can be so competitive that they don't have a chance to win.

"Lock the door and stay in your room. We'll figure something out. It might be as simple as you coming in tomorrow and eating a giant plate of crow."

When Krekorian hangs up, O'Hara takes the back stairs to the street. She heads a block down Houston to American Apparel, where she buys leggings, socks, a T-shirt and panties, then walks briskly uptown. There's a New York Sports Club on East Fourth between First and Second avenues, and in the ground-floor window, a dozen treadmills are lined up side by side, a woman running on each. Peering into the brightly lit interior from the street reminds O'Hara of that Hopper painting of the diner she finally saw in person last summer. The women on the treadmills are like the customers at that diner. Although they're only inches apart, each is stuck inside her lonely city head.

O'Hara's discount Riverdale membership doesn't apply in Manhattan, but the manager cuts her a break. After changing into her new leggings, O'Hara climbs onto a Lifecycle, sets the machine on 3 and starts chugging. Despite the discovery of McLain's van and the bloody mattress inside, O'Hara doesn't buy McLain as the killer. Someone in town three weeks doesn't dump a body in East River Park. There are people living here their whole lives who don't know it exists.

After a couple of minutes, O'Hara's cheeks and the back of her neck turn beet red. Then she starts to sweat. Ten minutes later, her hair and T-shirt are soaked, and she still doesn't see McLain as the perp, although she concedes to herself that if Pena had trained in the park, McLain could have found out about it from her. She bumps the setting on her bike to 6, then 9, then 11. By the time she hits 14, her thighs are on fire and sweat rolls off her nose.

When she gets back to her motel room, the hysteria is gone, sweated out like a fever. Still dripping, O'Hara sits at her desk and stares at the timeline on her worked-over piece of HoJo stationery. The only white space on either side is in the upper-left-hand corner of the back page. She uses it to write herself a three-line note.

> *Don't worry what other people think.*
> *Finish what you've started.*
> *You've earned the right to believe in yourself.*

Twenty minutes later, O'Hara sits in her Jetta on Forty-fourth, and stares through her windshield at the red awning of the Harvard Club. She calls the club from the car, and a Pakistani-sounding voice picks up at the front desk. "Got a question," says O'Hara. "I'm making a delivery first thing in the morning. How early does your service entrance open up?"

"Six a.m."

"Thanks, Captain. And where is it exactly?"

"The building runs from Forty-fourth to Forty-fifth. The service entrance is on Forty-fifth, just east of a restaurant called Yakitori Taisho."

O'Hara drives through Fifth, turns up Madison, then back on Forty-fifth. She double-parks in front of a steel black door and waits. When a uniformed porter steps out and lights up a cigarette, O'Hara gets out of her car, and when he rubs out the sparks beneath his shoe and steps back inside, O'Hara reaches the door before the lock can catch. She holds it barely open for a minute, then steps inside.

O'Hara takes the service elevator to the fourth floor and walks down a quiet corridor whose light green carpet and striped wallpaper look like they haven't been replaced in decades. Room

411 is at the southern end of the building, near the guest elevator. A cart loaded with soap, towels and toilet paper is parked beside the open door. O'Hara knocks lightly and shows her gold shield to a frightened rail-thin maid. According to the big white pin attached to her uniform, her name is Yvonne. She speaks very little English.

"Did you clean the room this morning, Yvonne?"

The woman shakes her head. "Estelle," she says.

"Is she here tonight?"

The woman nods and points at her feet.

In the basement, a female crew of international refugees stand beside an industrial-sized dryer, warming themselves as if around a campfire. Estelle is big and blond and eastern European. "I clean fourth floor every Thursday for year," she tells O'Hara.

"Did you see the man staying there this morning?"

"No."

"You sure? He used to come here with a young girl. She was nineteen, slim, short black hair, very pretty. You ever see her?"

"I never see her *or him*."

"What time do you get here in the mornings?"

"Six a.m. Work eighteen hours and never see them."

"They don't spend the whole night?"

"Nothing to clean. The man buys room but never stays. He is perfect customer. I want more like him."

O'Hara tries to reach Naomi on her cell but gets voice mail, and doesn't feel she can risk calling the house if there's a chance that Delfinger is there. For the third time that day, O'Hara crosses the Triboro and gets on 95, and an hour later rolls back through the white gates of Delfinger's private neighborhood. She parks a couple of houses beyond his and walks back to his driveway. Compared to the city, the suburban night is three shades darker and ten degrees colder.

O'Hara stops at the top of the driveway between Delfinger's Mercedes and his wife's Lexus. From where she stands, she can see the top and bottom of the staircase in the two-story entranceway and has a direct view of the lamp-lit living room, which looks like an idle stage set between acts. Because the single light is at the back of the room, it takes O'Hara a minute before she sees Delfinger, no more than twenty feet away, standing at the window. For more than five minutes, Delfinger, a glass of red wine in his hand, doesn't move. He just stands there and stares out at the night, and O'Hara, having seen no evidence of anyone else in the house, starts to panic.

What if Delfinger found out about O'Hara's visit this afternoon or her call to Naomi an hour ago? If he killed Pena, he could kill his wife too. To O'Hara's relief, Naomi Delfinger enters the living room. Cradled in her arms is one of her daughters, and the comfortable way she stands beside her husband convinces O'Hara that Delfinger is not aware of her visit or phone call. Naomi takes her husband's glass in exchange for a sleeping toddler, and Delfinger carries her out of the room and up the stairs. When they disappear down a second-floor hallway, O'Hara calls Naomi's cell again. From the other side of the bay window, she watches Naomi jump in alarm and rush into the kitchen.

"Naomi, it's Darlene O'Hara."

"I know who it is," whispers Naomi. "Stop calling me."

"I'm in your driveway. I need to talk to you."

"Are you crazy? Daniel is upstairs. You can't do this to me."

"It's very important. You got to think of a reason to get outside. Quickly, he's coming down the stairs now."

From the driveway, O'Hara sees Delfinger reach the bottom of the staircase. Through his wife's phone she hears his footsteps on the wooden floor of the foyer and the tiles of the kitchen. "Naomi, it's eleven o'clock," he says, his voice as loud and clear as if he's talking into the phone himself. "Who calls this late?"

"Andrea," says Naomi into the phone. "I doubt you left them in my car, but I'll run out right now and take a look. I insist. It's no trouble at all."

Crouched between the two cars, O'Hara sees the side door open and Naomi run out in her slippers. Even in the dark, Naomi looks different. She's angry and she's scared, but not like she was during the afternoon. There's a glint in her eyes. "You won't be happy till you get me killed?"

"I'm sorry to be doing this," says O'Hara. "But there's something I need to know. Does your husband keep a place in the city?"

"Yes," says Naomi, her breath turning to steam in the cold. "I always knew he was cheating. Finally I hired an investigator. He found the place six months ago. Daniel still doesn't know I know. But I think he realized he was being followed."

"Why didn't you tell me about the apartment this afternoon?"

"I already told you too much."

"Naomi, I need that address."

44

Building 972, on the west side of Second Avenue, between Fifty-first and Fifty-second, is a shitty little tenement sandwiched between two generic Irish pubs. At three in the morning, both are still dispensing desperate cheer, and from across the street, where she has been parked for hours, O'Hara can see down the wooden length of the nearly identical and parallel bars. Every twenty minutes, a skinny old scarecrow takes a break from drinking himself to death to have a smoke. When he flicks his butt north, O'Hara notices the new awning of the candy shop three doors up. Is this, wonders O'Hara, where Pena bought the chocolate malt ball Lebowitz picked out of her teeth?

At three-thirty, a car pulls up behind her. O'Hara walks to the open window and places a hand on Krekorian's blocky shoulder. Krekorian responds with the exasperated look a parent gives a beloved daughter who has just gotten kicked out of her third school in a year. "This is it, Darlene. It ends tonight no matter what."

"Understood," says O'Hara. "You get the warrant?"

"What do you think I've been doing—getting a foot massage in Chinatown? I just the left the chambers of Judge Carl Kochanski. I told him we had reason to believe this apartment contained evidence of a murder. At three in the morning, that was good enough for Kochanski. He covers midtown east. If it doesn't pan out, maybe our friends Lowry and Callahan don't ever have to hear about it."

The two cross the street and step into the cramped vestibule. Take-out menus and business cards for locksmiths are stuffed into the casing for the buzzer. Above it, inside a cracked glass box, the names of tenants are spelled out in white plastic letters. The missing *i* and *g* from Higgins and the *k* from Baginski lay on their backs alongside dead flies and roaches at the bottom of the box. For 4C, there's no name.

O'Hara woke the super three and a half hours ago, just to make sure he was around. Now she does it again. Rubbing sleep from his eyes, he emerges from the basement and leads them up carpeted wooden stairs smelling of mold. When they reach 4C, O'Hara hands rubber gloves to the super and Krekorian and pulls on a pair herself.

"Like I told your partner, I haven't been in this apartment since Ivers moved in. Never had any reason to."

"He goes by Stan Ivers," O'Hara tells Krekorian. "According to our friend here, he's going through a nasty divorce and got the place so his kids would have somewhere to visit him. He says Ivers pays the rent in cash, six months at a time."

The super stretches a key from a hernia-inducing ring, turns over two bolts and follows Krekorian and O'Hara into the overheated apartment. In the dark, the radiators hiss like sprinklers, and O'Hara can smell the countless coats of cheap paint cooking in the damp heat.

Behind them, the super hits a switch, and an overhead light goes on in the tiny shabby kitchen just inside the door to their right. There are no signs of cooking. In the sink are a couple of glasses and a dirty ashtray, on the counter an empty bottle of Cuervo and box of Froot Loops. The only thing in the refrigerator is a month-old carton of Tropicana.

"Don't touch anything," O'Hara tells the super.

Krekorian turns on another light, and their eyes adjust to the blaze of colors in the living room. The room is small and as shabby as the kitchen, but Delfinger has dropped some cash on a bright green couch with purple pillows and a pink shag rug the same color as the Froot Loops. Behind the couch, three teenybopper posters are taped to the wall. O'Hara watches just enough MTV to know that the girl on the left, a diamond glinting in her navel, is Britney and the girl on the right, also wearing a cut-off T-shirt, her jean skirt unbuttoned to reveal her bikini bottom, is Christina Aguilera, but not quite enough to place the pasty rapper between them. From the baby blue tracksuit, fat Rolex and gold chains, she guesses he's some Eminem wannabe. Then she notices the diamond-encrusted dollar sign lighting up the center of the chains and the DANNY BOY written in gold script, and when she looks under the baseball cap sees that the face is twenty years too old for an up-and-coming pop star.

"Recognize him?" asks Krekorian.

"Daniel Delfinger," says O'Hara, "a forty-three-year-old tax attorney, also apparently known as Danny Boy."

Like the living room, the bedroom looks directly into the soot-covered wall of the neighboring building, and with all the windows closed tight, the radiator hiss is louder and the paint smell stronger. A flat-screen TV, stereo and a DVD player face a platform bed. The bright green bedspread and stuffed animals, including a nearly lifesize Pink Panther, are reflected in the screen. In the corner stands a tripod and on the night table are a couple cellophane packets from the candy shop. One is empty, the other half filled with green jelly beans.

O'Hara and Krekorian search for the camera that goes with the tripod. They scour the closets, cabinets and drawers, as well as the dirty space beneath every piece of furniture, and soon both are sweating profusely. When there's no place else left to look, O'Hara walks over to the small video player, on the stand beneath the TV, hits EJECT, and a small cartridge pops out. "Turn off the lights," she says. "Maybe we don't need the camera."

When O'Hara turns on the TV and hits PLAY, Consuela's face fills the screen. The high-definition close-up shows the down on her cheeks and neck, along with every pre-adolescent blemish. When the lens pulls back, Consuela bounces on the bed on her knees. Like her pop heroes, she wears a cut-off T-shirt and the same low-riding jeans she had on in her mother's apartment two days ago. The stuffed dinosaur and kangaroo sitting behind her against the headboard look like spectators.

"Show us your new tattoo, Con," says the off-screen adult voice of Daniel Delfinger. Consuela stops bouncing and turns around to let the camera zoom in on the patch of red skin just above her jeans. Inside it is a crude amateurish copy of the tattoo Francesca got in Williamsburg. "Does it still hurt, baby?" asks Delfinger.

"A little," says Consuela. Her high-pitched voice sounds even younger than eleven.

"What do the letters stand for?" asks Delfinger, a lawyer leading a witness.

Consuela twists her shoulders until she almost faces the camera and reaches her left arm around her waist. Then she points a chipped red fingernail at the *T*, the first of the six letters inside the heart, and says, "This." Slowly moving her finger from *H* to *B* to *D* and *B*, she says, "Hynie . . . Belongs . . . to . . . Danny . . . Boy."

"Is it true," asks Delfinger with a nasal trill, "what the tattoo says?"

"Yes."

"How do I know?"

"Because it is."

"Are you ready to prove it?"

Consuela turns away from the camera, and an off-screen female voice very much like hers says, "It's OK." When Delfinger's naked body steps into the frame, O'Hara realizes the voice is Moreal's and that she is the one aiming the camera.

It takes twenty-three minutes for the video to play out, but the heat and the smell and knowing that they're standing in the room where the film was made make it feel many times longer. O'Hara makes it to the end by concentrating on her timeline on that piece of HoJo stationery, running it through her mind again and again like a voice-over as she finally fills in the rest of those missing one hundred eleven minutes.

"Eight-thirty p.m.," says O'Hara to herself, "Pena leaves McLain at her apartment and walks north up Orchard. She passes Joe's Drapery and Adrienne's Bridal Shop, turns west on Houston in front of American Apparel and walks down the stairs into the Second Avenue subway stop. She catches an F train to Thirty-fourth Street, runs to Penn Station and catches a 1 train uptown. At 9:06, she gets off at Broadway and 168th Street. Eight minutes later, she, Moreal and Consuela enter the 168th Street station on the downtown side, and just over an hour later Pena buys two CDs at Tower Records at Broadway and East Fourth. But first she delivers her two little sisters to 972 Second Avenue. At 10:30 Pena meets her girlfriends at Freemans, and when they leave, she stays. Not, like she tells them, because she wants to hook up or because she's avoiding her old boyfriend, but because she's waiting until it's time to pick up her girls."

As O'Hara fills in the last empty spaces in her timeline, something else occurs to her. When Pena was stripping and hooking, what she was really doing was trawling for johns for Consuela and Moreal. If the bent was there, one date was enough for her little-girl routine to draw it out. "Mister, I see you like to pretend you're doing little girls. How would you like to do the real thing?"

The video answers a lot of questions, but not who killed Pena. According to the time code in the upper-left-hand corner of the screen, the killer couldn't have been Delfinger. He was here doing something else.

45

Eventually, techs arrive to secure the crime scene. They replace the locks on Delfinger's door and add new keyed ones to the six wall-facing windows. It's seven in the morning before O'Hara and Krekorian can leave. By then the sun is halfway up on a hopeless December Friday. At the corner of Fifty-second and Second, the newspaper vending machines have been restocked, and dueling covers trumpet McLain's arrest. MAN WITH A VAN, shouts the *Daily News*. HELL ON WHEELS, the *Post* shouts back. But pedestrians hustle by obliviously. O'Hara feels as if the city slipped overnight into a parallel universe— one that is operating on lousy information and false hope.

O'Hara and Krekorian climb into their Impala and enter the park through Central Park South, grateful that the bitter cold has kept joggers to a minimum. North of the reservoir, Krekorian pulls off the road onto the muddy grass and rolls down his window.

"You were looking pretty Irish in there," says O'Hara.

"Was I? Trees look a lot better to me than people right now."

"They don't fuck up kids."

Krekorian looks over the tops of the trees and inhales the

cold park air through his nose, trying with each breath to undo the time in Delfinger's apartment. "There's something I never told you about my mom," he says. "She was a junkie too. Not a street junkie like the mother of those two girls, but a proper upper-middle-class, suburban junkie.

"The worst part," continues Krekorian, "was I was her *favorite*. That meant I was the one who got to go to her long list of quack doctors and plead for more quaaludes and vicodin. I used to pick up the prescriptions on the way back from basketball practice. And I was the one who got to hear about what a horrible person and loser my old man was and how she should have married any of the dozens of other better men who had also wanted her. It's amazing I didn't become a fag."

"You became a cop instead," says O'Hara. "Same difference."

"I figured if an Armenian American housewife from Montclair can turn herself into a junkie, why can't I become a cop?"

From the park, they drive to a diner on 102nd and Broadway, where they get a booth by the window and drink coffee until the Radio Shack across the street opens. When it does, O'Hara buys a cheap tape recorder, some batteries and three ninety-minute tapes for forty-three dollars. "Save the receipt," says Krekorian, before he turns on the flasher and they race up Broadway to Washington Heights.

This time, Consuela and Moreal are at school, and Entonces looks almost relieved to see them. With O'Hara suspended, Krekorian is the one who tells her she is under arrest for the murder of Francesca Pena. When he reads her her rights, she waves them away with the back of her hand, and makes no objection when O'Hara, hoping to God the thing works, sets up the tape recorder on the kitchen table. No physical evidence connects Entonces to the crime, and with all the trouble she's in, O'Hara knows her only chance is to bring this in wrapped up like a Christmas present.

"This is Detective Krekorian, and I'm here with Detective Darlene O'Hara and Tida Entonces, who has just been arrested for the murder of Francesca Pena. Entonces has waived her right to an attorney and is talking to us in the kitchen of her apartment at 251 Fort Washington Avenue."

O'Hara whispers a question into her partner's ear, and Krekorian redirects it to Entonces. "Tida, when did you discover what Pena was doing with Consuela and Moreal?"

"Five hours before I killed her," says Entonces, as if already looking back at her life from a great distance. "Francesca had taken the girls for one of their special sleepovers. All that afternoon, before Francesca picked them up, the girls acted nervous and squirrelly. They talked to each other in code, and Moreal teased her younger sister about something scary that was going to happen to her. When I asked about it, they giggled and made faces, and I put it out of my mind. I figured nothing bad could happen to them if they were with Francesca.

"I went to sleep early, but after less than an hour, I sat up in a panic. Something terrible was happening. I could feel it. There's a clock beside my bed. It was 11:05. I went into the girls' room and looked through their drawers until I found the diary I bought for Consuela."

"You still have it?" asks Krekorian.

"Yes. Can I go get it?"

"Witness requests permission to get a diary," says Krekorian into the machine. "Detective Krekorian accompanies her as she retrieves it."

Entonces returns, clutching a small white dime-store diary. Embossed on the cover in gold letters is MY JOURNEY. Entonces sits down and flips some pages, stops and reads: "Had fun with M and F and DB. I can't believe DB is forty-three. He sure doesn't act it."

Entonces turns a page, and when she reads again, O'Hara tries not to see her daughter and Delfinger on the flat screen. "Mister Dinosaur is so cute. I'm so lucky. DB buys us nice things."

"I thought the presents came from Pena," says Entonces, then turns a couple of pages and reads again.

"DB says I'm his favorite. He likes me even more than M but says the other things I do aren't enough anymore. I'm scared, but Moreal says it only hurts a little."

"Why didn't you call the police?" asks Krekorian.

"Then I lose the girls forever," says Entonces, looking away. "Children's Services would blame me, and they would be right. I OD'd three times. Why didn't I die? My girls would have been better off. Now they have nothing. Now they *are* nothing."

"How about the tattoos?" asks Krekorian for O'Hara. "What did you think about them?"

"Francesca, Moreal and Consuela, they all got the same one, so I thought it was a good thing. In the back of my mind, I was always waiting for the other shoe to drop, for Francesca to get tired of us and move on. The tattoos, I hoped, meant that wouldn't happen. They'd be sisters forever, no matter what."

"What did you think the tattoos meant?"

"Love. Money. Happiness. All the good things."

"What did you do after you read the diary, Tida?"

"I called Pena and told her I knew what was happening. She told me to meet her at a bar on Rivington. I took a subway downtown, but I didn't go in. I waited outside. When she left I followed her. At the corner, she got sick. I came up from behind and hit her with a hammer."

"You brought a hammer with you?"

"I brought a lot of stuff," says Entonces with something close to a smile.

"You planned what you were going to do before you got downtown?"

"Mostly, but some things I added while I waited. It was fifteen degrees that night and I was out there for a long time, but I never got cold. There was a construction site around the corner with plywood around it; I opened up a space between two sheets with the other side of the hammer, pulled her inside and dragged her to the back. I taped her mouth, tied her hands and feet and cut off her clothes. They even had a light, so I could see what I was doing. The best part was when she opened her eyes and realized that no one was going to help her."

"You raped her with the hammer?"

"With a broomstick I found lying around. Just like the cops did to Louima. It was the first thing I did. I wanted her to know what it felt like."

"What did you do with it?"

"Burned it. In the incinerator down the hall."

"How about the man? Why didn't you kill him?"

"All I had were his initials, DB. I had to find out who he was, where he worked. Pena told me all that, and I was still waiting for my chance. But if it had to be only one, I'm glad it was her. She found us. Acted like she was saving us, then she turned my girls into whores."

"How long did you torture her?"

"A long time. When she stopped breathing, I was angry."

O'Hara takes out her Radio Shack receipt, writes "phone # ?" and slides it over to Krekorian.

"Tida," says Krekorian, "we checked Pena's cell phone records. There's no call on it from you."

"She had two phones," says Entonces. "a nice orange T-Mobile and a prepaid one like they sell in my neighborhood. I found them both along with two CDs and the keys to her boyfriend's van when I went through her bag. I kept the CDs for the girls and threw the phones in the sewer."

"We only found one of them," says Krekorian. "The T-Mobile."

"Look again."

"You used the van to move the body?"

"She told me he always parked it near Tompkins Square and what it looked like, and I found it in less than five minutes. It was like God was helping me, and it was all meant to happen. I knew about that park by the river and that closed-down bathroom from when I was using. By the time I got home the girls were already there in bed. I knew it was DB, who must have panicked when Francesca didn't show up, and put them in a cab. But I acted like I didn't know. I tried to act like I didn't know anything. That afternoon, I dropped the van in long-term parking at Newark Airport and caught a bus back to the city."

"Were you the one who called in the tip?"

"I had to. Your partner over there was getting too close."

"Tida," says Krekorian. "We got to go downtown now."

"Who's going to be here when my girls come home? Who's going to be here for my babies?"

46

To get out of the neighborhood without a ruckus, O'Hara and Krekorian don't cuff Entonces until they get her in the backseat, and Krekorian doesn't hit the siren until they're off Fort Washington Avenue and swooping down through the shadow of the George Washington Bridge. On the West Side Highway, Krekorian grabs the empty right lane and stays on it, clocking ninety as O'Hara looks out over the guardrail at the black ice bobbing in the lethal water and Jersey City and Hoboken loitering on the far bank. At Fiftieth, the siren clears a lane through the crosstown traffic, and in minutes Krekorian pulls up sharply in front of 479 Lexington. O'Hara offers to sit in the car with Entonces, but Krekorian waves her off. "No need to cheat yourself, Dar," he says. "With what's on that on video, Delfinger won't be crawling through any loopholes."

O'Hara rides the elevator thirty-seven floors to the offices of Kane, Lubell, Falco and Ritter, where business is brisk and the meter is running. A large pretty black woman in a headset looks askance at O'Hara from behind a mahogany bunker.

"I need to see Daniel Delfinger," says O'Hara. "Immediately."

"I'm afraid that's not possible. He's with clients." But forty-three thousand dollars per year buys only so much loyalty, and when O'Hara flashes her gold shield, the receptionist's eyes light up.

"Let's go," says O'Hara.

Hips swaying and heels clicking, the receptionist leads O'Hara through a frosted-glass door and down a short corridor. She stops in front of the closed door of conference room 3. "Knock and step inside," says O'Hara. "I'll be right behind you. And don't leave until I do." The door opens on a long, very expensive-looking table around which a thick white document is being giddily passed from hand to hand like a big fat blunt. A petite smartly dressed brown-haired woman has just delivered a financial quip that plays off the heady tension of the imminent closing, and the tittering gradually comes to a stop as the room processes the unscripted intrusion.

"Give me two minutes to take care of this," says Delfinger, jumping out of his chair. "I'll be right back."

"Unlikely," says O'Hara. She steps forward to meet him in the middle of the room and shoves him hard facedown on the table.

Initially, Delfinger's clients are nearly as shocked as he is. But they get over it. As O'Hara cuffs him and reads him his rights, the clients and receptionist wear the same excited close-lipped smiles. They are far more grateful for the workplace drama than put out by the disruption.

"What are you arresting him for?" asks the brown-haired woman.

"I'll leave that to Danny Boy," says O'Hara as she pulls him off the table by his pinned wrists. But Delfinger, already damaged beyond repair, is barely capable of making a sound, let alone forming a word.

With the receptionist leading the way like a majorette, O'Hara shoves Delfinger down the hallway and into an elevator. As soon as the doors close, Delfinger's legs slide out from under him. O'Hara bends to his ear, says "Fuck you" and leaves him on the floor. On the thirty-fifth floor, a man in a suit steps halfway into the car, says "Daniel?" and bolts. Two floors below, a messenger shows no such misgivings and steps casually over Delfinger's splayed legs.

When they reach the lobby, O'Hara grabs one of Delfinger's legs and pulls him across the black marble floor on his ass. Just before Delfinger reaches the curb, Krekorian steps through the door, and yanks him to his feet. He throws him in the backseat with Entonces. Then he hits the siren and pushes through the thick Midtown traffic.

After a couple of silent blocks, O'Hara twists in her seat to face the two handcuffed passengers. "I need to apologize to both of you," says O'Hara. "I got so caught up in the activities of the morning, I forgot to do the introductions. Tida, the man on your left is Daniel Delfinger, but his really close friends call him Danny or Danny Boy or simply refer to him by the initials DB. And, Daniel, the woman on your right is Tida Entonces. If the last name is familiar, it's because she's the mother of your two girlfriends, Consuela and Moreal."

Delfinger looks at O'Hara in horror, but all he can get out

of his throat is a gurgling noise. By then it doesn't matter, because Entonces is attacking him like a schizo street cat, spitting and biting and scraping his face with the edges of her cuffs. "Why can't folks get along?" asks Krekorian. "Beats me, K." When Krekorian finally pulls over, Delfinger's glasses are broken and his face is in shreds. Krekorian stops the car and gets in back between the two of them, and O'Hara drives the rest of the way downtown. She gets on and off the FDR and turns onto Pitt Street. Cars and TV vans from half a dozen local networks are double-parked all the way up the hill, and milling in front of the precinct house are some twenty reporters from small papers and radio stations who lacked the clout to get inside.

"K., you make a call while I was dragging down Delfinger?"

"Not me."

As O'Hara works her way down the street, a piece-of-crap Impala exactly like theirs approaches 19½ Pitt from the opposite direction. When the homicide detective Patrick Lowry climbs out, the locked-out reporters surround his car and besiege him with questions.

"Is McLain your man?" "Have you got a confession?" "Does McLain have an alibi?" O'Hara and Krekorian realize the media crush has nothing to do with them.

With Lowry serving as a 360-pound decoy, O'Hara and Krekorian easily slip Entonces and Delfinger in through the back door. Even inside, the precinct is overwhelmed by reporters. O'Hara and Krekorian are able to get their two suspects to the fingerprint machine without anyone noticing except the desk sergeant, Kenny Aarons.

"What the hell you doing here, Darlene?" asks Aarons. "I thought you were suspended. We miss you, by the way."

"Just helping my old partner out on something."

"And what the fuck might that be?" asks Aarons. He eyes the two perps, one of whom is covered in blood.

"Give us a couple minutes, Kenny," says Krekorian. "We can't talk right now."

The new computerized fingerprint machine works only slightly worse than the old one. Despite the fact that Delfinger keeps sliding to the floor and Entonces has to be continually restrained from attacking him, they eventually get them both printed. As they wait for the machine to spit out copies, Krekorian wanders down the hall and sticks his head into the muster room. A podium has been set up in front, and Lowry towers over it, facing the standing-room-only crowd.

"How'd you find the van?" a reporter calls out from the back.

"We got a tip," says Lowry. "John Q. Public doing his job."

"Have you charged McLain yet?"

"No. We hope to by the end of the day."

"Why'd he do it, Detective?"

"Why do people ever do these things?"

"Dewey, I mean Lowry, is making his victory speech," Krekorian tells O'Hara when he gets back. By now, a couple dozen more scrub reporters have pushed and connived their way into the precinct. Those who can't get into Lowry's press conference in the muster room are backed up in the corridor. The end of the line is so close to the fingerprint machine that Delfinger is practically bleeding on their cheap suits.

As O'Hara and Krekorian try to figure out the best spot in this bedlam to park their suspects, the familiar figure of Sergeant Callahan pushes toward them through the clogged corridor. Callahan is not as happy to see O'Hara as Aarons. "You picked a hell of a day to come in and play detective again," he says. "But I don't even know why I'm talking to you, O'Hara. Your career is over." And then to Krekorian, "This isn't doing yours any good either."

"Sarge," says Krekorian, "before you go down in flames with Dewey in there, we got to tell you something."

"What the fuck are you talking about?"

"Dewey is the guy who ran for president against Truman in 1948."

"I know who Dewey is, you condescending college asshole."

"This is Tida Entonces," says Krekorian. "An hour ago we got her taped confession to the murder of Francesca Pena. She killed her because Pena was pimping her eleven- and thirteen-year-old daughters to this piece of shit over here, named Daniel Delfinger."

"What makes you think she's telling the truth?"

"For starters, she's the one who called in the tip on the van. It wasn't some eagle-eyed civilian like Lowry is telling them. It was her. She got the keys off Pena when she attacked her and knew exactly where the van was parked because she drove it there. Your choice. Stick with Lowry if you want, but this thing is tighter than a squirrel's ass. And one other thing, Sarge: I'm just an extra pair of hands here. This is all O'Hara, and when these reporters are through with her, she might decide to run for mayor."

Callahan's skills at police work are limited, but he's not color blind. And right now the sod under his feet looks a lot greener than the crabgrass down the hall. Shoving bodies out the way, Callahan fights back down the hall and into the muster room, where he works his way to the podium.

"NYPD can't be everywhere," says Lowry, as Callahan whispers in his ear, "but good citizens like the anonymous caller so crucial to this case can be our eyes and ears."

In the hallway, several reporters at the end of the line over- heard Krekorian's discussion with his sergeant. Now it's the small-time print and radio guys, whose audience wasn't big enough to get them past the velvet rope, who are closest to the story. Word of it races back through the line so quickly that even while Lowry stands at the podium, reporters turn their backs on him and rush the back door. In the scramble to locate a small red-haired female detective, few notice Lowry slip out a side door. But it doesn't escape the attention of observant reporters that when O'Hara is finally brought into the room and set up behind the podium, the same man who five minutes earlier stood beaming beside Lowry now stands just as proudly behind his suspended detective.

47

The cabins are set in a row on the bank of a steep hill. When O'Hara pushes through the door she can smell the damp air coming up from the frozen lake, and the stars and moon are bright enough to read the *Post*, if they let you read the *Post* up here. The thermometer beside the door reads minus seven.

O'Hara negotiates the stairs in her heavy boots and heads to the shed. In the far corner she finds the wheelbarrow, backs it out and with the bent wheel jouncing over rocks and frozen ruts, pushes it up the gravel road. Past the last cabin, the gravel becomes a mud trail, which climbs into dark woods, and a quarter mile later opens into a small clearing, whose missing trees are now a stack of logs covered by a green tarp. This is the part of the procedure O'Hara dreads the most, and to reduce the odds of an unwanted encounter with Mother Nature, she noisily stomps her boots and claps her gloves. Then she whips back the tarp like a magician and quickly fills the wheelbarrow with wood. Back at the cabin, Velma, a lush from the Seventy-third in Brownsville, helps her get the logs up the stairs, and Megan, a methhead from Patchogue, feeds them into the cast-iron stove, pausing at every opportunity to smile long-

ingly at O'Hara. O'Hara told her the day she arrived that
when it comes to cable, her tastes run to *The Sopranos*, not *The
L Word*, but like most guests here Megan is practiced in the
art of denial. "You see the flames licking those logs," she tells
O'Hara. "That's how I want to lick you."

Whatever, thinks O'Hara. Ignoring her butch admirer, she
climbs into her bunk, and reaches for the comfort of her mail.
She pulls out a card from the desk sergeant, Kenny Aarons. It's
a drawing of a squad car, and beneath it in big uneven letters:
"To Dar at the Farm." The drawing and penmanship are at the
level of a modestly talented five-year-old, but the thought of her
buddy Aarons putting crayon to paper on her behalf never fails
to produce a smile. If she ever makes it back to Bruno and Riverdale, she's going to have it it framed and hang it in her apartment. O'Hara is thinking about exactly where, when a counselor,
named Dougherty, sticks his bearded head into the cabin.

"O'Hara," he says, "you got a call."

O'Hara layers up again and steps back into the bright cold.
The moonlight, this way too fucking serious moonlight, O'Hara
thinks, misquoting Bowie, as she trudges past the neighboring
cabins with their chimneys pluming gray smoke. Perched on
the hilltop is the largest structure in the facility, whose name
is Hanover Woods, but is referred to by every cop who gets
sent there as the Farm. Careful not to trip over a table or chair,
O'Hara walks through the dark cafeteria and the room behind
it with the chalkboard where visitors are subjected to group
therapy and initiated into the mysteries of the twelve steps. In
a smaller room just beyond that, there is a soda machine and a

foosball table and the pay phone. O'Hara picks up the dangling receiver and hears Krekorian on the other end.

"What you up to, K.?"

"Not a whole lot. Sitting in the car with Loomis here, polishing off a slice from Stromboli's."

"What's on it?"

"Sure you want to know?"

"Not really. Tell me anyway."

"Peppers, meatballs and onions. And a delicate dusting of oregano."

"You were right. I didn't want to know."

Even after the arrest of Entonces and Delfinger and a week of worshipful coverage in the tabloids, O'Hara faced serious disciplinary measures from NYPD for defying her suspension, interfering with an ongoing investigation, and leaving the scene of a crime. The idea of making them go away by checking herself into rehab was actually Maître Dee Dee's, concocted during O'Hara's all-night celebration with Krekorian and Lebowitz at the Empire Diner. "Now that you're a celeb, baby girl, you gots to act like one," said Dee Dee. "And, besides, from where I'm standing, it wouldn't exactly kill you to go easy on the sauce for a few weeks."

Having said his piece, Dee Dee returned his attention to doling out and shaking the contents of O'Hara's fifth martini, while O'Hara concentrated on groping Lebowitz beneath the counter, and Lebowitz, who was honest-to-God shitfaced drunk for the second time in his life and grinning like an imbecile, did his best to stay mounted on his stool.

"Jewish boys, Dee Dee," said O'Hara as she ran her nose over Lebowitz's prominent Adam's apple. "What makes them so hot?"

"You mean aside from their shlongs?"

"Yeah, Dee Dee, aside from that?"

"Nothing."

"I heard that," said Lebowitz, clutching the counter with both hands as if he were riding the roller-coaster at Coney Island.

The next morning, reeking persuasively of gin and vermouth, O'Hara walked into the Seven and sat down across from her favorite sergeant, Mike Callahan. "The reckless behavior and insubordination were only symptoms," she told him straight-faced, her vicious hangover once again contributing much-needed ballast for her shameless bullshit. "The underlying problem that has to be addressed, and the sooner the better, is demon alcohol."

"The hardest step is admitting you've got a problem," said Callahan, and although he didn't believe a word O'Hara said, he was more than happy to play the fool. The way the media had been drooling over his renegade detective, NYPD was as anxious as O'Hara to resolve the matter gracefully. Twenty minutes later, Callahan came back with a proposal. If O'Hara agreed to four weeks at an accredited facility on NYPD's dime, her slate would be wiped clean—no suspension, no loss of pay, no lost vacation days. The following afternoon, O'Hara was on a bus to the Poconos.

"I have some news," says Krekorian as he swallows another bite of his slice.

"Is it good?" asks O'Hara.

"Not good or bad. It just is. Delfinger got murdered at Rikers this afternoon."

"Didn't those morons have him in protective custody?"

"Yeah—North Infirmary Command—but apparently it wasn't protective enough. An inmate slit his throat on his way back from the yard. He bled out in ninety seconds."

"A friend of Tida's from the neighborhood?"

"Doesn't look like it. Just some three-time loser already looking at life. Says he did it for the girls. Probably just wanted to feel like a hero. Like Loomis says, Rikers is a self-cleaning oven. And by the way, Loomis sends his regards."

When O'Hara gets back to her cabin, it's lights out. She climbs into her bunk and stares into the darkness overhead. The prison yard execution of a pedophile shouldn't cost her sleep, particularly after the video she sat through. But it does.

She thinks about Delfinger and Entonces in the backseat that morning and the primal fury with which Entonces attacked him after O'Hara introduced him as the "DB" in Consuela's diary. It reminded her of the time she and Axl watched a bluejay strafe a cat who had wandered too close to her nest. The outsized bird swooped down from the tree and attacked with everything she had: beak, feet and flapping wings.

Looking at Axl that day, O'Hara understood how the mother bird felt, but what O'Hara can't get out of her mind tonight is the look in Delfinger's eyes just before Tida pounced. That and the drowning sounds that came out of his mouth instead of words.

48

Three weeks later, an hour before dawn, Rick Helmsford, the ex-cop and recovering alcoholic who runs the Farm, gives O'Hara one last signature hug and puts her on the Trailways back to New York. O'Hara, who hasn't slept in two days, is out before the bus is back on the highway and doesn't open her eyes until the corkscrew descent into the Lincoln Tunnel.

Thanks to Walt and Rudy, O'Hara arrives in a highly sanitized Times Square. What little sleaze is left is sucking on a respirator in and around the Port Authority. O'Hara walks past a working girl in hot pants asleep on a bench, and slips into a concourse bar. At ten in the morning, as a janitor swabs the floor and ESPN reheats last night's highlights on an overhead TV, she washes out the chalky taste of all those AA meetings with a couple of ice-cold Amstels.

Fortified, she catches a 1 train to Riverdale, and without stopping at her apartment, gets in her car and heads down the West Side Highway. Grateful to have the Hudson on her right once again, she drives the length of the island, rounds the Seaport and takes the Manhattan Bridge into Brooklyn.

On a quiet street near Fort Greene Park, O'Hara finds

the house of Donna and Albert Johnson, the foster parents for Consuela and Moreal before the state returned them to their mother. Eleven Lafayette Street—O'Hara got the address from Nia Anderson at Big Sisters—is a warm, somewhat dilapidated row house, and Donna Johnson, who answers the door in a maroon sweater and black slacks, is a warm, somewhat dilapidated black woman in her early sixties. She deposits O'Hara in a large parlor with enough sofas and chairs to seat thirty, and when she reemerges from the kitchen, has a plate in one hand, coffee in the other.

"You got to try my plum tart," insists Johnson. "It's the only good thing I make." O'Hara, who hasn't eaten anything good in a month, needs little convincing.

While O'Hara tucks in, Johnson pulls a photo album from a shelf and sits beside her on the couch. "In the last twenty-three years, ninety-one children have lived in this house with Albert and me," says Johnson, the hand carefully turning the pages clenched by arthritis. "Every one of them had to go through their own little piece of hell to get here."

Johnson points at a skinny boy about six, who stares defiantly at the camera from the front stoop. "This young man is Arthur Henderson. He was with us five years. Now he works as a computer technician." O'Hara patiently sips her coffee, as Johnson points out a young girl who just got her high school equivalency, another employed as a teacher's aide and a third earning twenty-eight dollars an hour unloading planes at Kennedy Airport. "No doctors or lawyers yet. Maybe one day."

Eventually Johnson's finger stops under a picture of two

young girls, obviously sisters, their hair pulled back in tight braids. The younger one smiles shyly with her arm around the shoulders of her older sister, who raises two fingers behind the younger girl's head. "This bright mischievous girl is Moreal Entonces," she says. "And of course that's Consuela. It's not easy to look at this picture now, is it? Moreal was eleven, Consuela nine."

"Donna, what'd you think when Children's Services returned the girls to their mother?"

"Neither of us could believe it. Albert and I have been doing this long enough to know there's always going to be a bias for the mother, but Tida had been a junkie for twenty years and clean for six months. It was too soon by at least a year. And the worst part, both girls had turned the corner. After only ten months, they were doing better at school, better at home, better with the other kids."

"Then why did they do it?"

"I'm not sure, but I know a big part of it was Francesca Pena. She snowed Children's Services just like she snowed everyone else. And she went after it. She didn't just vouch for Tida; she wrote letters to her caseworkers and her probation officer, even wrote to our local fool congresswoman. And since those letters were coming from a student at a fancy school like NYU and a young woman who had turned her own life around, they were persuasive."

O'Hara and Johnson sit and stare at the two young sisters. Although the photo is two years old, Consuela's face looks hardly different than in the video.

"So what do you think will happen to Tida, Detective? I mean, after the jury decides that what she did was justifiable? Is she going to write a book? Do the talk shows? Am I going to see her on the couch beside Oprah? Is there even a chance she is going to get those girls back again?"

"No," says O'Hara.

"I wish I could be as sure of that as you," says Johnson. She wraps one warm fleshy arm around O'Hara and looks at her in mock alarm.

"Girl, I'm getting you another slice right now. You ain't nothing but skin 'n' bones."

49

From Fort Greene, O'Hara takes the BQE to the Grand Central, gets off at Astoria Boulevard and follows Twenty-third Avenue into a huge chain-fenced parking lot at the edge of the East River. At the end of the lot, a guard waves her onto an unnamed two-lane bridge, and she drives for more than a mile out over the water. LaGuardia Airport is so close on her right, the roar of landing planes is deafening and she can see a pier of lights directing pilots to runway 13/3.

In the watery tissue between the boroughs, ten miles from the Statue of Liberty, is Rikers Island, the nation's largest penal colony, built by the city on a 415-acre island of trash. Over the bridge, O'Hara heads down an eerily quiet street lined with aging brick jails, most of which have sprouted at least a couple of cheap modular additions. With its own power plant, bakery, chapels and hospitals, it's a world apart, and as Delfinger's violent demise illustrated, it's run by the inmates as much as the guards.

The island has ten jails. O'Hara parks near the Rose M. Singer Center, the only one that holds women. As she walks in from the parking lot, she can hear a newborn crying in the nursery, some lucky infant who got dealt a hand right up there with Moreal and Consuela and Marwan. Entonces has just finished a meeting with her public-appointed attorney in one of the closet-sized rooms near the visitors' lounge, and the guards have kept her there rather than return her to her cell. When O'Hara steps in, Entonces, wearing dark green scrubs, sits uncuffed at a small metal table.

"You look different," says Entonces.

"Been away."

"Me too."

"That's too bad about what happened to Danny Boy," says O'Hara.

"A crying shame."

"You put up a bounty?"

"Didn't have to lift a finger. Place like this is full of volunteers. From what I hear, guys were fighting over who got to do him."

"Still," says O'Hara, "getting to him in only two days is pretty quick."

Entonces shrugs. "You expect me to be sorry? Send flowers to his family?"

"Remember Moreal and Consuela's foster mom in Brooklyn, Donna Johnson?" says O'Hara. "I visited her this morning. A very nice woman. Bakes a helluva plum tart."

"Good for her."

"She told me the only reason you got your daughters back was Pena went to bat for you with Children's Services."

"She's right. Till Pena came along, I was just another unfit junkie mom. Who was going to listen to me?"

"And Pena didn't stop at phone calls, said Johnson. She told me Pena wrote letters, lots of them. And visited your caseworkers and met with your probation officer. I wondered why she went to so much trouble."

"We all know why," says Entonces, looking away from O'Hara at the colorless cement walls, smelling of sweat and disinfectant. "So she could take my beautiful children and turn them into whores. So she could sell my babies to people like Delfinger."

"And because she knew you'd go along with it."

"What are you saying? That twisted bitch played me like everyone else."

"Why go to all that effort to get them away from a place where they were finally safe and doing well, unless she knew for a fact it was going to be worth her while? That's what Delfinger was trying to tell me in the car, before you attacked him, wasn't it? The night you killed her, you probably swung by his place and picked them up yourself."

"You're crazy. Like I told you, he put them in a cab."

"Maybe. But how much of Delfinger's money was going to you, Tida? A quarter? A third? Whatever it was, it wasn't enough. Well, maybe at first. You could buy yourself a TV, some clothes. But not for long. And why should you get a cent less than Pena? Why should Pena get a dime? Moreal and Consuela were *your daughters. Your flesh and blood.* You carried those girls for nine months. You brought them into this world and could have died doing it, and some Puerto Rican yuppie shows up at the last minute and takes all the money? It was like you were getting screwed all over again, just like you have your whole life."

"Then you get it," says Entonces, turning from the wall and staring directly at O'Hara for the first time since she arrived. "I'm their mother. A mother has her rights."

50

On a sticky morning in late August, O'Hara leans against her rented Mitsubishi and watches gawky adolescent girls stagger around a cement track. The track, which is cracked and gouged and might once have been green, is behind the Arthur Alvarez Center for Juveniles. The facility, cut off from a treeless neighborhood of warehouses and outdated factories by a double-height barbed-wire-topped fence, is as bleak and institutional as Pena described.

In June, after prosecutors were made aware of the mother's active role in the prostitution of her daughters, Entonces copped a plea that will keep her off *Oprah* for the next ninety-nine years. O'Hara fell back into the routines of her work, the standard Seventh Precinct bullshit, ameliorated by the dependable ardor and affection of Lebowitz, who is already her longest-running relationship since the heartbreaking, bong-sucking fireman. Despite the satisfaction of seeing Entonces locked up for life, and the novel experience of actually having one herself, O'Hara is still haunted by the case, so much so that she has cashed in three vacation days and flown JetBlue to Chicago on her own dime to try to learn what turned a bright teenage girl into a psychopath.

Delfinger and even Entonces, O'Hara can comprehend. Unfortunately, she's encountered scumbags like them too many times not to. But Pena, at least the why and how of her, is as much of a cipher as the afternoon David McLain walked into the detective room and reported her missing. So instead of sharing a towel with Lebowitz and Bruno on Jones Beach, O'Hara watches juvenile delinquents jog around a steaming track.

Chicago summers come highly recommended, but the lake breezes don't reach here. At 6:45, it's pushing eighty, and the heat takes its toll, particularly on the heavier girls, one of whom veers off the track and pukes in the dust.

"All done, fatso?" asks a heavyset man with a flattop and a pink face. "Then get back out there. This isn't camp. No one cares how you feel." When O'Hara pushes off her car and approaches the man from the far side of the chain-link fence, he steers his contempt from the girls to her.

"Didn't you see the sign?" he asks. "Or can't you read?"

"I love to read," says O'Hara. "Got anything to recommend?"

She shows him her shield, then holds up two pictures of Pena: one as a Westfield High School freshman, the other an NYU sophomore. "Recognize her? Her name was Francesca Pena."

The man looks back over his shoulder to make sure no one is taking advantage of his inattention and slacking off. "Yeah," he says. "She's the girl who got murdered."

"How long have you worked here?" asks O'Hara.

"Too long. Can't you tell?"

"So you must have known her. She was here in the summer of 2001."

"No, she wasn't."

"But you recognized her?"

"I remembered her from the stories in the papers," says the man, looking over his shoulder again. "When they came out, I couldn't place the name or the face. But a lot of girls come through here, and in a couple years, at that age, they can look completely different. So I went through the records. Turns out, I wasn't so dumb after all. She was never here."

"But she described this place to a T."

"I wouldn't know about that," says the man, walking back toward the track. "But she was never here. You don't believe me, call Juvenile."

O'Hara drives back to the Econo Lodge and reads *USA Today* until the municipal offices open at nine. Then she calls the Department of Juvenile Justice, which sends her to its Custody Movement and Control Unit. When the latter confirms that Pena never went through its system, she calls the Board of Education and Elections, the Office of City Archives, the Postal Service, the Office of Public Assistance and the Food Stamp Office, the HIV/AIDS Services Administration and the Department of Health and Mental Hygiene. She often makes up to a dozen calls to each as she gets bounced from division to division, employee to supervisor.

O'Hara works the phone for four hours and gets exactly nothing. There is no record of Pena attending public school in Chicago. No record of her or Ingrid and Edwin Pena having lived there. No record of her parents voting in a city or federal election or receiving public assistance or food stamps. No record of Edwin Pena having been treated for AIDS at a Chicago hospital or succumbing in a local hospice. No addresses. No phone numbers. No utility bills. No certificates of birth or death.

O'Hara puts down the phone and pulls open the curtains. It's one in the afternoon, and there's a knot in her neck the size of a golf ball. For ten minutes, she squints at a glaring white parking lot that could be anywhere in America, except the one city she shouldn't have left. She thinks about Lebowitz and Bruno and feels like an idiot. Then she sits back down on the unmade bed and calls the Seven. The desk sergeant Kenny Aarons picks up.

"Kenny, I need you to run a check on someone, name of Ingrid Coppalano."

"Dar, where you calling from?"

"Chicago. It's a long story."

"Coppalano, as in Francesca Pena's mother?"

"Yeah."

"Ancient history, isn't it, Dar?"

"I know. It's embarrassing."

"Give me a sec. This computer's a piece of crap. Here we go—one arrest—DWI—4/27/99."

"Where?"

"Beacon, New York."

"Wonderful. She wasn't even in Chicago. I should have called you four hours ago."

"Dar, you can call me whenever you want, day or night. You should know that by now."

"Kenny, you're the best. What else?"

"Maiden name, Ingrid Falb. Married Dominic Coppalano in New Paltz, New York. I been hiking around there. It's beautiful."

"When?"

"Two summers ago."

"Not you, Kenny. When did Ingrid Falb become Mrs. Coppalano?"

"Twenty-two years ago and change—5/15/83—in Beacon, New York. Two years later, on 4/5/86, Francesca Falb Coppalano was born, also in Beacon."

"Jesus H. Christ."

"I say something wrong, Dar?"

51

When Aarons's voice drops off the line, O'Hara feels the need to be someplace cool and dark with a jukebox and a liquor license. The Indian woman at the front desk directs her to a Polish neighborhood of tidy single-family homes, where she parks in front of a tan brick tavern that looks like it was built to survive Armageddon. Inside it's as dark and dank and lovely as St. Patty's Cathedral, and Sinatra's slightly embarrassing cover of Petula Clark's "Downtown" wafts luxuriantly from an ancient Wurlitzer. Four for four, thinks O'Hara, like Jeter on a good day. With a pleasant lack of urgency she has not felt since the night McLain walked into the Seven, she sips her cold draft.

It's a good thing O'Hara isn't feeling rushed, because there's a fair amount to haul aboard. Starting with the most fundamental, Francesca Pena was not Francesca Pena. She was Francesca Coppalano and no more Puerto Rican than Bruno. She never watched her father waste away from AIDS because he's still alive, and when she arrived in Westfield, Massachusetts, for her first year of high school, she wasn't fleeing a Chicago barrio, simply moving from Beacon, New York. If a girl wants to reinvent herself, the first year of high school is apparently the most propitious time to do it, since colleges and prep schools aren't particularly interested in anything earlier. She would have needed fake middle school transcripts for her first day in Westfield, but how much scrutiny are they going to attract? "You don't by any chance serve food?" O'Hara asks the barkeep halfway through her second draft. Ten minutes later, he places a beige plate, circa 1960, in front of her on the bar, and O'Hara sees her luck is holding. On it are three slices of dark rye, two fat blackened sausages, a mound of potato salad and a dollop of sharp mustard. Not until her plate has been wiped clean by her last crust of bread does she consider how what she's just learned might have helped push Tomlinson over the edge.

She remembers Tomlinson's reluctance to surrender Pena's application and her anxiousness to get it back. Had she too discovered Pena was a fraud? If so, O'Hara can appreciate her alarm. What if everyone found out that Tomlinson, with her Ethiopian sculptures carved out of dung and Romare Bearden print, couldn't tell a chica from the barrio from a brat from Putnam County? For someone whose career was based at least in part on the politics of race and whose unwritten job description was keeping it real, that could be a serious problem. But the possibility that Tomlinson was fooled to the end appeals to O'Hara even more. It would mean that despite all Tomlinson's worst intentions, the woman was truly color blind.

O'Hara doesn't order a third beer. Instead she leaves a twenty-dollar tip for her twelve-dollar tab and drives back to the airport, where she watches travelers trapped between cities shuffle through the hushed limbo like zombies. With a two-hour wait for the next flight to New York, O'Hara buys a paper and camps out in Starbucks. There her mind circles back to Pena, and to her dismay she realizes that despite a truckload of revelations, she isn't an inch closer to understanding Pena and how she became who she was.

She recalls the wretched figure of Dominic Coppalano at the medical examiner's office and again at the memorial. What kind of father, she wonders, would let himself be expunged from family history to improve his daughter's chances of getting into college? Probably one so desperate to undo the undoable, he'd agree to anything.

After walking the equivalent of ten city blocks, O'Hara finds a screen listing departures. JetBlue's got a flight to Boston in forty minutes. If she catches it, she could be in Westfield tonight. Maybe with one last detour she could find out what the old man did to his daughter. Did he abuse her himself? Did he sell her to his friends just like Pena did with Consuela and Moreal? The gate is nearby and the line moves briskly enough for O'Hara to stand a chance, but as she nears the head of it, doubt, in the form of Kenny Aarons's voice, undermines her resolve.

"What the hell you doing, Dar?" he asks. "I thought we both agreed this was ancient history. Who cares what Dominic did to Francesca, and if by some chance you find out, are you then going to want to know what his old man did to him? You're a cop, remember, not a fucking social worker. Start unraveling all this crap, you won't be done till you're back in the trees, swinging hand over hand with the chimps."

Aarons's persuasive monologue is interrupted by a female voice from behind the counter. "Ma'am?" says an attendant. "Can I help you?"

"Yes," says O'Hara after a pause. "Yes, you can." And hands over her ticket and license.

O'Hara switches her flight, but not to Boston, and four hours later steps out of the terminal into a soft dusk. She has never been to this city before, but something in the air, simultaneously charged and laid-back, appeals to her immediately. She even likes the funky ten-year-old cabs lined up on the curb.

She slides into one, and on the way downtown, the radio plays a promo for an upcoming show at the rock-and-roll museum. She imagines a vast granite edifice like the Metropolitan Museum, but instead of Egyptian monuments and paintings by the masters, permanent exhibits for Aerosmith, Lynyrd Skynyrd and AC/DC and gives the new city huge props for that too. But soon the detached observations of a tourist are replaced by an unbearable tension, and by the time the cab pulls off the highway her palms are as sweaty as the guiltiest suspect's.

The cab winds through a neighborhood that resembles the Lower East Side on quaaludes. The twenty-something pedestrians move so languorously she can understand why there's a coffee shop on every corner. The cab drops her off at the address she keeps in her wallet, and she is buzzed into a scruffy six-story building. She rides the elevator to seven and knocks on the door. After an excruciating wait, a tall young man with a full red beard and a freckled forehead opens the door, and O'Hara, who barely reches up to his chest, throws her arms around him and doesn't let go. The name of this startlingly handsome young man is Axl Rose O'Hara. Darlene O'Hara is his much too young mother. And like Entonces said, a mother has her rights.

ACKNOWLEDGMENTS

For letting me hang out with them and so generously sharing their stories from on and off the job, thanks to Detectives Keith Flannery, George Taylor and Steve Nieves from the 7th Precinct Detective Squad, Detective Irma Rivera from Manhattan Homicide South and Detective Donna Torres from Homicide North. For crucial guidance and support, my editor, Claire Wachtel, and agent, Todd Schuster. And for bearing up under the stress and tedium, my wife, Daina Zivarts.

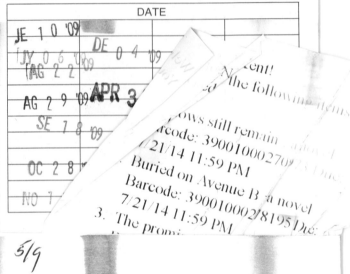